THE ULTIMATE PLANETS

THE ULTIMATE PLANETS

by Donald Goldsmith

Diagrams by Jon Lomberg

QPB®

The Quality Paperback Bookclub
New York

Byron Preiss Multimedia Company, Inc.
New York

An Original Publication of The Quality Paperback Book Club

QPB
1271 Avenue of the Americas, New York, N.Y. 10020

For information address:
Byron Preiss Multimedia Company, Inc.
24 West 25th Street
New York, N.Y. 10010

The QPB website is www.QPB.com

Byron Preiss Multimedia World Wide Website Address is www.byronpreiss.com

ISBN 0-671-01204-5
First printing: July 1998
10 9 8 7 6 5 4 3 2 1

Printed in the U.S.A.

Edited by Michael Sagalyn and Ruth Ashby
Managing Editor: Michele LaMarca
Editorial Assistant: Jeff Solomon
Photo Research: Tara Godvin
Cover Design by Steven Jablonoski
Interior Design by Dean Motter
Production by Joe Kaufman

CONTENTS

I would like to thank my friends and relations who helped me while
I was writing this book:

Marty Africa, Bruce and Kathy Armbruster, Sam Bader, Charles Beichman, Simon Bell, Arnie Berger, Aviva and Kenneth Brecher, Marianne Cohen, Pascal Debergue, George and Susan Field, June Fox, Marjorie and Victor Garlin, Jane Goldsmith, Paul Goldsmith, Rachel Goldsmith, Amy and George Gorman, Jerry and Marjorie Heymann, Gentry Lee, Doug Lin, Jon and Sharona Lomberg, Vince Mannings, Sally and Stephen Maran, Geoff Marcy, Lawrence Marschall, Tom McGuire, David Morrison, Alexander and Eleanor Orr, Tobias Owen, Merrinell Phillips, Astrid and Howard Preston, Jo Powe, Arlene Prunella, Sheryl Reiss, Anneila Sargent, Roy and Sara Schotland, Frank Shu, and Jesse Upton. At Byron Preiss Multimedia Company: Michael Sagalyn, Ruth Ashby, Tara Godvin, and Jeff Solomon worked to make this a better book.

■INTRODUCTION

Humans long to connect with the universe and to find meaning in the cosmos. These desires support our spiritual longings and undergird our efforts to understand nature. When we look to the heavens, we aim to perceive how we came to be here, on a modest planet that orbits an average star in a far corner of the Milky Way galaxy. We are an exploring species, curious and restless in our cosmic neighborhood.

When our descendants look back on the twentieth century, they will surely mark it as the time when humanity actually began to explore the solar system, the family of objects that orbit the sun. This exploration will eventually take human beings to other planets, and possibly even to planetary systems around other stars. For now and the near future, however, our hopes of learning more about the solar system rest with the fantastic automated spacecraft that we send on multi-billion-mile voyages to the most distant planets. Although astronauts may receive the publicity, our mechanical wanderers get the job done—a fact that often seems to diminish the glory of learning more about worlds beyond Earth. But a moment's reflection will show that in fact we deserve more credit, not less, for finding ways to explore by constructing representatives to go boldly into regions where no human has ever been.

This book describes the results of humanity's successful exploration of the solar system and the planets that orbit nearby stars. My hope is that you will join me on a short, sweet tour of the solar system and the worlds beyond, reveling in that marvels so far discovered, and anticipating more exciting discoveries in the millennium to come. I cannot promise you fame or fortune from this journey. To paraphrase Thomas Jefferson, the trip will neither put money in your pocket nor grow hair on your head, but it will allow you to understand the great cosmic quest on which humanity is now engaged: the search to understand how we came to be here, and how we fit into the cosmic scheme of things. Enclosed with this book is a CD-ROM containing additional images, games, and descriptions for your further amusement and enlightenment. Let your spirit rise to meet the worlds that circle the stars, and you will receive a psychic reward, one that enriches your soul by allowing you to share in the knowledge that others have striven so hard to obtain.

—Donald Goldsmith
Berkeley, California   June 1998

CHAPTER ONE

THE BIRTH OF THE BLUES

Four and a half billion years ago, in a dark corner of a dense interstellar cloud, the sun and its planets swirled themselves together. A nearby disturbance—perhaps the explosion of an aged star—ruffled the gases of a subclump within a giant cloud of gas and dust, starting a chain of events that gave birth to our solar system. Within the subclump, which spanned a diameter thousands of times larger than the orbits of all the planets, the density of matter increased as the result of the disturbance from outside. As a result, the subclump began to contract, as each of its parts exerted gravitational attractive forces on all the other parts. Because the random motions of its molecules proved insufficient to resist these gravitational forces, the subclump shrank within a few hundred million years, by a factor of a thousand, concentrating matter at its center, squeezing its core by gravity until the sun began to shine, while leaving hundreds of much smaller, nonluminous objects in orbit around the newborn star.

On the third sizable object outward from the sun, the local conditions proved favorable for the origin and growth of creatures capable of reproduction and evolution. Life appeared early in Earth's history, just a few hundred million years after the planets coagulated from the gas and dust orbiting the sun. Earth's first 3 billion years saw the oceans teeming with trillions of sea creatures, none of which had more than microscopic size. Among their other achievements, some of these tiny creatures, floating in the seas of Earth, produced the greatest pollution ever seen on this planet. These blue-green bacteria took enormous amounts of oxygen from seawater, processed it, and discharged it into the air, changing Earth's atmosphere from a nearly pure-nitrogen composition into the nitrogen-oxygen mixture we find today, a mixture that allows ourselves and all other animals to maintain metabolic activity by breathing the oxygen-rich gas that surrounds us.

Four billion years after the sun and its planets had formed, creatures larger than microscopic life began to appear on Earth in increasing numbers and a variety of forms. During the Cambrian explosion, almost 600 million years ago, the immediate ancestors of all vertebrate animals appeared in the oceans. Within another few hundred million years, large plants and insects had colonized the Earth's land masses, followed by vertebrates a hundred million years later. Just under 200 million years ago—a time when more than 95 percent of the Earth's current history had already passed—the age of dinosaurs began. For more than a hundred million years, thunder lizards ruled the Earth, the largest and most successful creatures yet seen on our planet, while our mammalian forerunners, shrewlike darters fearful of passing instantly from predator to prey, strove to find insects in the savannas and forests.

Sixty-five million years ago, a five-mile-wide asteroid collided with the Earth. The impact sent so much dust into the stratosphere that the skies grew dark for months. All the dinosaurs died; our ancestors, by happy accident, survived to claim ecological niches suddenly free from reptilian domination. Before long, mammals flourished in amazing variety, overspreading the land, returning to the seas as whales and dolphins, taking to the skies as bats. A few million years ago, our hominid ancestors appeared on the plains of Africa. Before long, they had evolved into Cro-Magnon and what we call modern human beings, creating societies in which curious individuals set out to uncover not only their own evolution but also the story of the universe that brought us here.

Like all epics concerned with the distant past, the retelling of how part of the Milky Way turned into ourselves starts by covering enormous amounts of time, then slows its pace as it approaches the epoch of human history. If we imagine the journey from the birth of the sun to the present day as a drive from San Francisco to Times Square in New York City, we use three thousand miles of highway to represent 4.5 billion years of cosmic history. Life on Earth arises as we cross the high Sierras, less than one-tenth of the way to New York. Microscopic, single-celled organisms ride with us across the Great Basin, the Rockies, and most of the Midwest;

multicellular life appears only long after we have crossed the Mississippi River and are speeding through Ohio. The age of dinosaurs begins in eastern Pennsylvania and ends in the outer New Jersey suburbs; hominids come into existence as we cross the Hudson River; Neanderthal man holds sway half a block west of Broadway; and the Great Pyramid in Egypt rises ten feet from our journey's end. In this analogy, an average human lifetime covers only about three inches, a short span in which each of us can join the great voyage of life on Earth.

Understanding the Solar System

The last inch and a half have been golden for human understanding of the cosmos. A thousand years from now, our descendants will recall the second half of the twentieth century for humanity's first exploration of the family of objects that orbit the sun. That family includes nine planets; their satellites or moons; a host of smaller objects called asteroids, each with its own orbit around our star; swarms of nearly countless meteoroids, miniature asteroids many smaller than a pinhead; and perhaps a trillion comets, frozen snowballs containing the oldest and most pristine material in the solar system. Our spacecraft have visited seven of our eight neighbor planets, have passed by several asteroids for close inspection, and have flown by the most famous of all comets, the one named after Edmond Halley. Within the next few years, our robot explorers will bring us more information about Jupiter, Saturn, and their moons, as well as about the red planet Mars, for centuries the focus of human imagination in the search for extraterrestrial life.

Before we leap into the results that our exploration has revealed, we owe it to ourselves—and to those who did the hard work—to look back over the long effort to understand the basic frame of the solar system, a struggle that testifies to human patience, curiosity, and ingenuity. No single person, living on the Earth's surface and admiring the lights that spangle the night skies, could alone conceive of the basic sizes and motions of the objects that form the solar system. Generations of astronomers, curious and enjoying a taste for debate, spun theories to explain the changing patterns in the skies. Once they realized that these hypotheses could be tested against what actual observations revealed, their devotion to this scientific method led them to our basic understanding of the solar system: The sun occupies the central position, while the planets, moons, asteroids, meteoroids, and comets orbit around it. Though this simple statement turns out to require some modification, it remains basically correct, as well as utterly, fundamentally shocking. The notion that we live on a planet that hurtles through space could hardly be more contrary to human intuition. Let us pause to admire the mental processes that led to the recognition of this counterintuitive concept as true.

Keep Your Eyes on the Skies

Modern citizens have no time to watch the stars. Even if they choose to look, their heavenward gaze encounters the veils of city-born light that civilization casts over itself, eliminating the dark skies that allowed—indeed encouraged—our predecessors to admire the stately progressions of the heavens. From lifetimes of observation, our ancestors knew directly, in a way that modern learning tends to exclude, what was going on in the sky.

They saw the sun by day, and the lesser lights of night, rise in the east, swing slowly across the sky, and set in the west. These motions demonstrated beyond reasonable doubt that the entire dome of heaven rotates around the Earth, carrying with it the sun, moon, and stars. Only one point on the dome remains stationary: the pole that marks the point of intersection between the overarching dome and the imaginary axis around which the dome of heaven rotates. Objects close to this pole never rise or set, but simply perform circles around the pole that keep them always above the horizon. Most of the objects in the sky, including the sun and moon, are sufficiently far from the pole that the rotating dome of heaven carries them alternately above and below the observer's horizon.

You never gain something but you lose something, as Thoreau said. Long-vanished generations of humans found it obvious and reassuring that we live beneath a sheltering canopy of the sky, which carries celestial objects as it turns. Today, everyone knows (more precisely, everyone is taught) that not the sky but the Earth does the turning. In actuality, most of us have lost the comfort of "knowing" that the sky encloses the Earth, without deriving much benefit from a correct knowledge of our place in the cosmos.

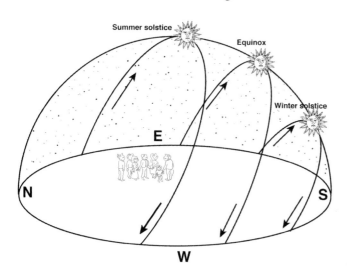

Astronomers, who have internalized both the old and the new ways of looking at the heavens, still find the concept of a dome of heaven to be useful in telling one another where to look for a particular object at a given season and time of night. They have named the dome of heaven the celestial sphere, and the stationary pole the north celestial pole, even though they know full well that the sphere and pole exist only as mathematical constructs, relics of a time when everyone imagined the Earth to lie at the center of the universe.

Ancient cultures imagined that the dome of heaven turned around the Earth once each day. At different seasons, the sun had different locations on this dome, and therefore rose to greater or lesser heights above the southern horizon.

When our ancestors contemplated the turning heavenly dome, night after night they found five peculiar objects among the several thousand points of light that they could see in the clear dark skies of Earth. Although these objects, like the stars, are carried by the dome of heaven from east to west, they seem to possess an additional will to wander, as they slowly change their positions on the heavenly dome, measured with respect to what bygone astronomers called the fixed stars, whose positions remain immutable through human lifetimes.

These five planets have a name that derives from the Greek word for "wanderer." Though the word may be Greek, the recognition of objects that wander across the turning bowl takes us much further back in time than the ancient Greek civilization, to at least two thousand years B.C.E. Furthermore, this earlier date refers only to written records that have survived the flood of time. We may suppose, with entirely reasonable near certainty, that even in cultures without writing, intelligent men and women, well endowed with a capacity for memory, noticed and discussed the seven objects—the sun, the moon, and the five planets—that continuously changed their positions among the stars. To many societies, the existence of these mysterious objects showed that the number seven has mystical properties, worthy of, for example, numbering the days of the week.

The Sun Moves Around the Celestial Sphere

Of the seven wandering objects, the sun clearly had the greatest role to play. Since the changing positions of the sun in the sky governed our ancestors' lives, an ability to guess and eventually to predict the sun's position on the sky bowl had important repercussions in the lives of farmers and hunter-gatherers.

What changes does the sun undergo during the course of a year? Today, only a few astronomy buffs can describe the simple rule that describes these changes, though they must have become evident to anyone who studied the skies carefully. Every year, the sun makes a circle around the celestial sphere, gliding against the background of fixed stars by 1/365 of a complete circle every day. The Greeks named the sun's path around the dome of heaven the ecliptic, because this path plays an important role in the occurrence of eclipses of the sun and moon. If we conceive of the celestial sphere as rotating around the Earth once each day, we must imagine that the sun slides slowly around the ecliptic, constantly losing a little ground to the fixed stars, so that each day the sun remains above the horizon a bit longer—just about four minutes—than the stars do.

Endowed with excellent memories, our ancestors knew perfectly well which stars lie in a given direction in the sky, even when sunlight prevents us from seeing the stars. They knew this because the sun's yearly circle around the celestial sphere eventually allows observers to see all the stars under nighttime conditions. In winter, star groups such as Taurus and Orion ride high in the night skies, while constellations such as Scorpius and Virgo lie in almost the same direction as the sun, and so

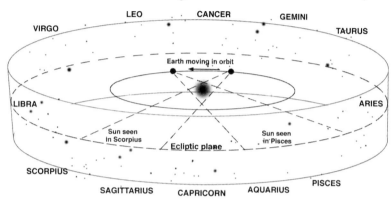

remain invisible because they are "up" only during daylight hours. Six months later, when the sun has orbited halfway around the ecliptic (in modern terms, because the Earth has circled halfway around the sun), Scorpius and Virgo dominate the night skies, while Orion and Taurus have become invisible in their turn.

As the Earth moves in orbit, the sun appears to circle the celestial sphere along a path called the ecliptic, spending about one month in each of the twelve constellations of the zodiac.

In naming the constellations, European civilizations have inherited the designations given nearly four millennia ago in ancient Babylonia and passed on through ancient Greece. The Greeks called the twelve constellations that surround the ecliptic the zodiac, meaning "animal path," because almost all of these star groups were given names of animals or humans. Ancient Babylonians matched regal characteristics with the monarch's "birth sign," the zodiacal constellation in which the sun lay at the time of his birth. Modern astrological newspaper columns still follow this tradition, despite the fact that today everyone's birth sign is "incorrect": Slow changes in the Earth's orbit have shifted the times when the sun occupies a particular zodiacal constellation by about a month and a half from what was true when astrology began. This fact has barely put a dent in astrologers' incomes.

How can we describe the position of the zodiac, and thus of the ecliptic that the zodiac contains, on the celestial sphere? The north celestial pole, the stationary point on that sphere that we can see, lies directly above the Earth's north pole. In exactly the opposite direction, directly above the Earth's south pole, lies the south celestial pole, never visible from northern latitudes because it never rises above our horizon. Halfway between the north and south celestial poles lies the celestial equator, the points on the sky directly above the Earth's equator. The belt of Orion straddles the celestial equator—quite convenient for seafaring Polynesians, who knew that if Orion's belt appeared directly overhead, they must be on our planet's equator, though they used different words to describe their correct conclusions.

If the sun's ecliptic path happened to coincide with the celestial equator, the Earth would be far less interesting than it has turned out to be. The sun would then always occupy some point on the celestial sphere halfway between the two celestial poles. Even though the sun would still slide around the celestial sphere each year, losing four minutes per day with respect to the stars, on every day the sun would follow the same path across the sky, rising exactly in the east, reaching the same maximum altitude directly to the south at local noon, and setting directly in the west. No seasonal variations would occur in the sun's path across the sky, and nothing would change in the way that the sun shines on Earth. Summer, winter, and other seasons simply would not exist, and quite possibly life on Earth would never have evolved the fantastic variety we find now.

The Tilt of the Earth Gives Rise to the Seasons

In actuality, however, the sun's ecliptic path does *not* coincide with the celestial equator. Instead, the ecliptic and the celestial equator are tilted with respect to one another, like giant hoops that intersect at just two points. This difference arises from the fact that the Earth's axis of rotation, instead of being perpendicular to the plane of the Earth's orbit around the sun, tilts by 23 1/2 degrees away from the perpendicular. (To the ancient Babylonians, we also owe our units of angular measurement: 360 degrees make a full circle, so 90 degrees form a right angle and 45 degrees half of a right angle.) If the angle of tilt were zero, and the Earth's rotation axis were perpendicular to the plane of its orbit, then the two hoops of the ecliptic and celestial equator would merge to form a single circle around the celestial sphere. In reality, however, the two hoops diverge, and on only two days of the year—the equinoxes that occur close to March 21 and September 23—does the sun happen to occupy a position on the celestial equator, simply because its ecliptic path crosses the equator on those two days. On those two equinoxes (the name means "equal night"), the sun rises directly in the east and sets directly in the west, spending 12 hours above the horizon and 12 hours below, for observers all over the Earth.

The other days are different. Either the sun lies to the north of the celestial equator (between March 21 and September 23) or to the south of it, that is, closer to the south celestial pole than to the north celestial pole. On the summer solstice, on June 21 or 22, the sun reaches its maximum northward deviation on the celestial sphere, 23 1/2 degrees away from the celestial equator. On that date, any northern-hemisphere observer will see the sun's maximum altitude above the southern horizon exceed the equinox altitude by 23 1/2 degrees. The sun will rise to the north of east, set to the north of west, and remain above the horizon for well over 12 hours. Six months later, at the winter solstice, the sun rises to the south of east, sets to the south of west, and reaches a maximum elevation above the southern horizon 23 1/2 degrees less than the equinox value.

All seasonal variations in the climate arise from the sun's changing ecliptic positions through the course of a year. The days in spring and summer, when the sun spends more than 12 hours above the horizon and rises to a greater-than-average height above the horizon, tend to be warmer than those of fall and winter, when the sun is up for significantly less than 12 hours and falls far short of even its equinox height above the southern horizon. To make sense of the preceding rules, observers located south of the Earth's equator must substitute "south celestial pole" for "north celestial pole" and "height above the northern horizon" for "height above the southern horizon." These observers also find that spring, summer, fall, and winter occur half a year out of phase with the seasons in the northern hemisphere. What we call the summer solstice in northern latitudes marks the beginning of winter south of the equator.

That Lesser Light: The Moon

Just as impressive as the sun's motion around the celestial sphere is the moon's, which repeats not once each year but once each "moonth," or month, as we now call it. Today we know that the Earth and moon each orbit the center of mass of the Earth-moon system. However, since the Earth has 81 times more mass than the moon, that center of mass lies inside the Earth, though not at the Earth's center, and we lose little accuracy in imagining, as our ancestors did, that the moon circles the Earth while the Earth remains stationary.

Because the moon produces no light of its own, it shines only by the sunlight it reflects. The moon, like the Earth, therefore always has a lit half and a dark half, of which we see different proportions as the moon orbits. At full moon we see all of the moon's bright side and none of the dark half, whereas at new moon, half a month later, we see none of the lit side, and cannot see the moon at all for a day or so. At what we still call first quarter and last quarter of the lunar cycle, halfway between new moon and full moon or between full moon and new moon, we see half of the moon's lit side and half of its dark side. Month by month, this cycle has repeated itself more than 50 billion times, impressing our ancestors with the rhythmic growth and decay of the full moon. The moon takes 27 1/3 days to orbit once around the Earth. However, since both the Earth and the moon are orbiting the sun, the moon must complete a bit more than a full orbit in order to regain the same position with respect to the sun and Earth. As a result, 2 1/6 days more than an orbital period, or 29

1/2 days, must elapse for the moon to complete a full cycle of its phases.

As the moon orbits the Earth, it too appears to circle the celestial sphere. The moon's path around this imaginary sphere corresponds neither with the ecliptic nor with the celestial equator, though it lies much closer to the former than to the latter. The moon's trajectory tilts from the ecliptic by only 5 degrees, so if we again imagine two giant hoops, one for the moon's trajectory around the sphere and one for the sun's ecliptic path, the hoops nearly coincide—but do not. Their near coincidence means that the moon always lies within 5 degrees of the ecliptic on the sky. Hence the twelve constellations of the zodiac, which spread for more than 5 degrees on either side of the ecliptic as they embrace it, always encompass the moon as well as the sun.

Twice each month, the moon's motion causes it to intersect the ecliptic. *If, and only if, this crossing of the ecliptic occurs at the time of full moon or of new moon, we shall have an eclipse.*

This explains why the Greeks gave the name "ecliptic" to the sun's path: Eclipses happen when the moon lies on the ecliptic at

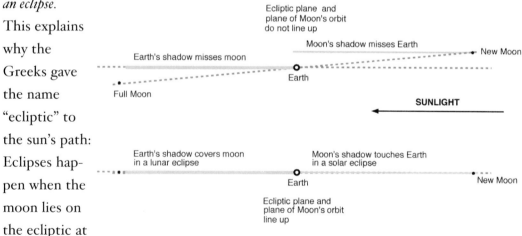

Because the plane of the moon's orbit tilts with respect to the Earth's orbital plane around the sun, the moon's shadow at the time of new moon usually misses the Earth, and the Earth's shadow at full moon usually misses the moon.

full moon or new moon. An eclipse at new moon will be an eclipse of the sun, when the moon passes directly between the sun and Earth, and blots out sunlight from the parts of the Earth's surface on which as the moon's shadow falls. In contrast, an eclipse at full moon must be an eclipse of the moon, when the Earth blocks sunlight from reaching the moon, and we see the moon nearly disappear as it passes through the Earth's shadow.

The Planets

The third and least among the motions visible on the turning celestial sphere, fraught with complexity and interest, are the movements of the five lesser objects that the ancient Greeks called planets. These five objects—Mercury, Venus, Mars, Jupiter, and Saturn—also remain within the constellations of the zodiac, never wandering far from the ecliptic. Like the sun and moon, the planets usually slide backward on the celestial sphere; that is, they move slowly from west to east, in the direction opposite to the turning of the sphere.

The most reasonable explanation for the motions of these seven moving objects (sun, moon, and five planets) seemed to be that each of them resides on a different spherical shell or sphere that rotates around the Earth. Closest of these shells must be the moon's, since the moon has the most rapid motion; next comes Mercury's, then Venus's, then the sun's, because the sun moves once around the celestial sphere during the course of a full year. Outside the sun we find Mars, Jupiter, and Saturn, which take approximately two, twelve, and thirty years, respectively, to circle close to the ecliptic. Farthest from Earth is the fixed stars' sphere, which turns once around the Earth every day, carrying with it the inner spheres. On this outermost sphere the stars eternally maintain their positions with respect to one another. In this way, eight spherical shells, each one (except for the largest) nested inside others, could explain the basic motions of the stars, planets, sun, and moon.

But exceptions to these rules governing the planets' motions do appear. From time to time, each of the five planets ceases its usual eastward motion and then, for a few days or weeks, moves in the opposite direction, from east to west on the celestial sphere. Ancient astronomers called these motions retrograde: backward in comparison to the usual movement of the planets. No one could ignore the planets' retrograde motions, which, for Mars, Jupiter, and Saturn, occur when the planet is best placed for viewing, rising at sunset and remaining all night in the skies. Even though no motion could be seen during the course of a single night, a comparison from night to night soon reveals that the planet has reversed its usual direction of motion against the starry background. The planets' retrograde motions cried out for an explanation, and received one—first, a highly inventive but incorrect model that held sway for more than a thousand years, and later, a correct explanation that appeared during the sixteenth century C.E.

Ptolemy's Model of the Cosmos

Attempts to explain the planetary motions had to provide a rationale not only for the general west-to-east movement of the objects that moved against the background of fixed stars, but also for the occasional, exceptional, east-to-west retrograde motions of the planets. For those who intuitively believed that the Earth must be stationary at the center of the universe, this duality of motion created an immense problem. They could quite easily imagine that each of the planets, as well as the sun and the moon, moved on its own transparent, crystalline spherical shell, centered on the Earth, with each sphere at a different distance from us and the celestial globe of the stars most distant of all. But they then had to imagine that each of the planets performs an additional excursion on its own spherical shell, in order to explain its retrograde motion.

Ancient astronomers embraced this task. Generations of work, with one astronomer building on the theories of his predecessors, eventually produced the master work of Claudius Ptolemy, who lived in Alexandria during the second century C.E., the astronomical books known to western cultures as *Almagest* ("the greatest"). Ptolemy's *Almagest,* whose Arabic name reflects the fact that Islamic astronomers kept learning alive after the decline of the Roman Empire, dominated astronomical thinking for more than a millennium, not only in the Islamic world but also throughout Europe, once scholars began the recovery of ancient learning lost during the dark ages. In this complex work, a cosmos of intricate workings emerged, of circles within circles, each carefully calculated in order to reproduce, as faithfully as possible, the observed motions of the sun, moon, planets, and stars.

Ptolemy's model of the cosmos was utterly wrong, fatally flawed by the error of imagining the Earth to lie at the center of the universe. But scientific conclusions often prove wrong. Far more important, in the sweep of human understanding of our surroundings, was the fact that Ptolemy and his predecessors strove to correlate their mental picture of the cosmos with what they observed. This attempt lies at the heart of what scientists do: They observe, they speculate, they incorporate those speculations in coherent mental models, and then test their models against further observations. To be sure, this approach was slow to emerge. During the millennium after Ptolemy, not much of this testing went on, and Ptolemy was taken to be the last word in astronomical knowledge. Eventually, however, the scientific approach prevailed, and new observations replaced the Ptolemaic model of the cosmos with the correct one. The struggle to find a better model for the planets' motions, and to show how and why it provides a better explanation, is one of the great triumphs of the scientific explosion that gained full force as the Renaissance drew to a close. Only when leading thinkers—though hardly the average citizen—had come to accept the new and improved model could it be said that humanity had discovered the solar system.

THE DISCOVERY OF THE SOLAR SYSTEM

Four and a half centuries ago, a small fraction of the intellectual segment of a minor constituent of the human population learned that a Polish churchman, publishing from his deathbed, had proposed a theory—for which he had no proof whatsoever—that the Earth does *not* occupy the center of the universe. This theory was slow to gain adherents; even today, most people have never heard of it, or reject it if they have. But the hypothesis adduced by Nicolaus Copernicus has turned out to be correct. Verified as well as any scientific theory can be, Copernicus's claim and its implications have sunk deeply into the consciousness of vast numbers of humans. The effect has been to dethrone ourselves physically and psychologically from our once assumed role as masters of the cosmos—except, of course, when we forget that we live on a speck of dust orbiting an inconspicuous star in a galaxy with nearly a trillion stars.

Copernicus became a canon (a minor official of the Catholic Church) with the freedom to devote many of his waking hours to the contemplation of the heavens. Born in 1473, twenty years after Johannes Gutenberg produced the first book printed with movable type, Copernicus went to Italy at the end of the fifteenth century to complete his education. He then returned to Torun (called Thorn by its former German-speaking inhabitants), a small city in Poland, where he spent months in intense concentration on the astronomical problems that had engaged his attention since his student days. Highly influenced by what we would now call mystical longings, Copernicus became dissatisfied with Ptolemy's model of the cosmos because it gives the sun no special place in the dynamics of the heavens, making it just one of the objects moving around the stationary Earth. Drawing on his conception of what "ought" to occur in a perfect cosmos, Copernicus became convinced that the sun, and not the Earth, *must* occupy the center of the motions. This may not be the way that scientists work today, but Copernicus's hunch turned out to be right.

The Copernican System

Like Ptolemy, and indeed like all astronomers before the seventeenth century began, Copernicus was completely devoted to the concept that all celestial objects must move along circular paths. Celestial objects were supposed to be perfect, and any deviation from circular motion would represent an unthinkable diminution of those objects' perfection. Hence when Copernicus envisioned a new, sun-centered picture of the cosmos (unknown to him, the ancient Greek philosopher Aristarchus had suggested this model nearly two millennia earlier), he could only suppose that all objects, now including the Earth, moved in perfect circles. The circles might appear in combination, as in the case of the moon circling the Earth as the Earth circles the sun, but nothing but circular motion could be contemplated.

But celestial objects do *not* move in perfect circles. To match the model with observations of the sun, moon, and planets, Copernicus's model, like Ptolemy's, turned out to require "fudge factors"—small circles called epicycles added as deviations from larger circular paths. In fact, Copernicus needed even more of these small epicycles to make things fit. Copernicus saw, however, that his model provided a better explanation of the retrograde (backward) motions on the sky observed for the planets, though not for the sun or moon. If each planet circles the sun at a different rate, with Mercury moving the most rapidly and Saturn the most slowly, then each of the planets will either overtake Earth (as is the case for Mercury and Venus) or be overtaken by our planet (for Mars, Jupiter, and Saturn). In either case, when one planet overtakes and passes another, we observe a temporary reversal in the planet's usual apparent motion against the backdrop of stars. You can observe a similar sort of retrograde motion whenever you drive on a highway and overtake cars moving more slowly: Those cars will appear to move backward against the background of a distant landscape during the few moments before and after you pass them.

Copernicus's sun-centered model had another virtue, not quite so apparent and carrying with it an enormous drawback. If the Earth proves to be "just another planet," not motionless but eternally circling the sun, then the explanation of day and night could much more reasonably be assigned to the Earth's own rotation than to the rotation of the outermost celestial sphere. Copernicus's model thus not only dethroned the Earth from its central position but also gave it a dual motion, of rotation once a day and revolution around the sun once a year. Central to Copernicus's thinking, in his model the glowing, life-giving sun became the majestic center of the cosmos, the sphere of the stars that no longer needed to turn, but could instead

remain immutably at rest.

In a culture and an era dominated by traditional Catholic theology, Copernicus's ideas seemed—and were—revolutionary in all senses. Copernicus, knowing this well, delayed the publication of his masterwork, *De Revolutionibus Orbium Coelestium* ("On the revolutions of the heavenly bodies"), until he was about to pass beyond the reach of secular authorities, and saw the first copy as he lay on his deathbed in 1543; he probably failed to note that it contained a preface by a would-be helpful prelate,

Nicolaus Copernicus (1473–1543) rediscovered the concept that the sun occupies the central point of the solar system.

Osiander, emphasizing that the new model was entirely theoretical. Copernicus's fellow astronomers immediately recognized the significance of the new model, though most of them refused to accept it, preferring the Ptolemaic wisdom. Because the struggles between Catholics and Protestants tended to put the latter in favor of a "literal" interpretation of the Bible, the Copernican, sun-centered cosmos received a much more favorable reception in Catholic areas than in Protestant regions of Europe. Martin Luther, the founder of Protestantism, inveighed mightily against those fools who would make the Earth, not the sun, move, when the Bible clearly states that the sun stood still for Joshua. In contrast, for more than half a century, Jesuit astronomers found Copernicus's model highly intriguing.

To most of the few European thinkers who deeply contemplated the operation of the heavens, Copernicus's model had little to recommend it, and seemed to contain a fatal flaw. Opinions varied as to the importance of the sun and the desirability of imagining it as the fixed center of the cosmos, and as to whether the turning celestial sphere made better sense than a stationary one. But if the Earth moves around the sun, why don't we see changes in the stars' positions in the sky as we view them first from one side of the sun and then, six months later, from the other side?

Copernicus recognized this difficulty and furnished the correct explanation: All the stars are so distant from the Earth that our yearly motion has almost no effect on how we view the stars. Detection of the parallax effect, the apparent change in a star's position that arises from the Earth's annual revolution, had to wait for three centuries, when telescopes and measuring instruments finally allowed astronomers to observe the results of the Earth's orbital motion. By then, Copernicus's model had long since triumphed, and the only people doubting that the Earth does not occupy the center of the cosmos were—and remain—those who have never heard of such an outlandish, counterintuitive concept or the man who brought it to the world's attention. Those who have accepted Copernicus's basic concept refer to our immediate neighborhood as the *solar* system, a community centered on the sun, around which orbit the planets, their moons, and a multitude of lesser objects.

A Century of Solar-System Astronomy

During the last quarter of the sixteenth century, the greatest astronomer of Europe was Tycho Brahe, a Danish nobleman who had grown fascinated with the heavens as a young man and abandoned the legal career his guardian planned for him. Tycho (called by his first name in most historical circles) eventually acquired his own island from the king, where he built an observatory that was the wonder of his age, capable of measuring the positions of objects in the sky with the finest precision attainable in that pre-telescope era. To understand the motions of the heavens, Tycho offered a conservative middle ground between the models of Ptolemy and Copernicus: He proposed that all the planets *except* the Earth circle the sun, while the sun itself, "carrying" all the planets around it, circles the stationary Earth. With a few adjustments, this Tychonic model could fit observations of the sun, moon, and planets as well as either Ptolemy's or Copernicus's.

Observations were Tycho's special skill. He had grown to love astronomy from early studies of a "supernova," a new star in the otherwise unchanging starry sphere; in fact, he had demonstrated by careful observations that this object, which appeared in the year 1572, must lie farther from us than the moon does. Without articulating it, Tycho had stumbled onto a key principle of science. To achieve the greatest success, scientists must make not a single good observation, but rather repeated, accurate observations, as frequently and as exactly as possible. This principle replaces the older belief, which dates back at least to Aristotle, that one good look at the situation should reveal its correct explanation to a powerful mind.

Apart from his model of the cosmos, Tycho made no significant theoretical contributions to astronomy, though his observations of the supernova of 1572 cast doubt on the belief that nothing in the realm of the "fixed stars" could ever change. Tycho's great legacy lies in the observations he amassed through decades of careful observation and notation of the positions of the sun, moon, and planets with respect to the stars. This treasure store devolved on the man who finally understood the planets' motions, Tycho's one-time assistant Johann Kepler.

A German from Swabia, Kepler learned of the Copernican system at the university in Tübingen from a professor who taught the model with gingerly caution, perfectly aware that the authorities had no love for this newfangled hypothesis. Kepler seized on it immediately and never doubted thereafter that the sun, not the Earth, lies at the center of the cosmos. Even more mystically inclined than Copernicus or Tycho, he wrote an early book attempting to explain the arrangement of the planets' orbits by using what mathematicians call the perfect solids (there are just five of these: the cube, tetrahedron, octahedron, dodecahedron, and icosahedron, each characterized by a set of identical faces and of identical angles at which the faces meet). Kepler proposed that each of the five spaces between the orbits of the six planets that he knew (Mercury, Venus, Earth, Mars, Jupiter, and Saturn) has exactly the right size to accommodate one of the five perfect solids. This explanation attests to the ongoing belief that the heavens must be perfect, and that the order of the cosmos reflects divine principles which humans have a chance to discern through years of study.

Kepler's effort to explain the number of planets and their distances from the sun proved premature by at least four centuries, for we still have no good explanation of why the sun has the number of planets we find, or why their orbits have the sizes they do. His imaginative undertaking attracted attention from astronomers of high repute. Tycho had left Denmark in a fit of pique and settled in Prague as the Imperial Mathematician to the Emperor Rudolph. There in the year 1600, he hired as his assistant the still youthful Kepler (who, lacking Tycho's forceful personality and aristocratic connections, had experienced trouble finding and keeping even a post as a high-

Johann Kepler (1571–1630) first realized that the planets move in elliptical orbits around the sun.

school teacher). Perhaps from envy of Kepler's superior mathematical abilities, Tycho denied him access to his observational records, occasionally providing a tidbit of planetary orbital data as the mood struck him. All came right for astronomy, however, when Tycho suffered an untimely death after one of the long banquets that punctuated life in castle circles, and apparently let his sense of propriety deny him a journey to the private chamber to which even the emperor must go by himself. Just a year after arriving in Prague, Kepler found himself Tycho's successor, though his salary went unpaid. With Tycho's observations at his complete disposal, he settled down for long periods of patient mathematical analysis, and eventually produced the correct description of how the planets orbit the sun.

After years of attempting to find combinations of circular orbits that would fit the observed positions of planets in the sky, Kepler reluctantly abandoned the concept of circular motion, to which he had previously been as firmly wedded as Copernicus or Ptolemy. Tycho's observations convinced Kepler that *every planet orbits the sun along an elliptical path*. An ellipse is a sort of stretched circle, defined by specifying two points inside it, called the foci (the Latin plural of the word focus), and by requiring that from every point along the ellipse, the sum of the distances to these two foci must remain the same. If the two foci coincide, the ellipse will be a circle with a single center; if they do not, the ellipse will be longest along its major axis, the line that passes through the two foci, and will be narrowest in the direction perpendicular to that line. For each of the planets' orbits, the sun occupies one of the two foci, while the other contains nothing but space, though it plays an equal geometric role. In all the planetary orbits, the two foci are relatively close together, so the orbits deviate only slightly from being circular. As a result, the discovery of their ellipticity had to await Tycho's compilation of accurate observations and Kepler's keen and determined mind.

Kepler also recognized that in order to explain what Tycho had recorded, he must abandon not only circular motion but also the related belief that each planet moves at a constant speed. Instead, as Kepler realized, each planet moves more rapidly when closer to the sun, more slowly when farther away. Today, thanks to Newton, we can say that the planet's motion keeps it from falling into the sun, and the speed of this motion must increase as the distance decreases. Kepler brilliantly deduced the exact relationship between a planet's speed in orbit and its distance from the sun. If we imagine a line connecting the planet to the sun, that line sweeps over equal areas in equal amounts of time. For this to occur, the line must move more rapidly when it is shorter, less rapidly when it is longer.

Kepler's first book about the planets' motions, published in 1609, drew immediate praise and attention from the few dozen people who knew what he was talking about. Though his reputation grew among the scientists of Europe, Kepler's fortunes slowly declined with the advent of a new emperor and the coming of the Counter-Reformation that made his Protestant beliefs a political handicap in the Austrian Empire. Never ceasing his astronomical labors, Kepler moved from Prague to Linz, where he discovered a third "law" describing the planets' motions, to rank with the elliptical-orbit and equal-areas-in-equal-times rules. Unlike the general statements made by his first two laws, Kepler's third rule compared the motions of the different planets. Kepler's quest to find God revealed in the geometry of the heavens, which had once led him to conceive of the five perfect solids as interplanetary spacing devices, now helped him to perceive a lovely mathematical relationship between the planets' orbital periods and their distances from the sun.

Kepler perceived that the imaginary line joining the sun to a planet sweeps over equal areas in equal intervals of time.

In analyzing these distances, Kepler had to deal with the fact that each planet's distance from the sun changes slightly as it moves around its elliptical orbit. Gone were the circles that named a single distance for each planet; in their place were the ellipses Kepler had found. To deal with this issue, Kepler took for each planet's distance the *semi-major axis* of its orbit, which is half of the major axis that spans the long dimension of its ellipse. This semi-major axis

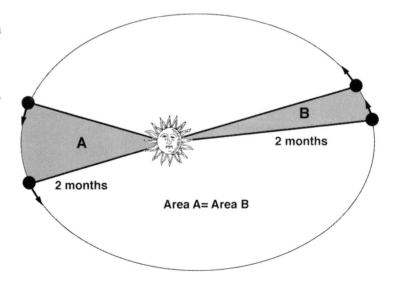

almost exactly equals the planet's average distance from the sun.

If we assign the Earth's semi-major axis a value of 1, Mercury, Venus, Mars, Jupiter, and Saturn have orbital semi-major axes equal, respectively, to 0.4, 0.7, 1.52, 5.2, and 9.5. In Earth years, these planets' orbital periods span approximately 0.24, 0.7, 1.9, 12, and 30. Kepler saw that the *squares* of the orbital periods are proportional to the *cubes* of the orbital semi-major axes. Jupiter, for example, has an orbital period (11.8 years) whose square (139.2) almost equals the cube (140.6) of its semi-major axis. As more accurate orbital data became available, Kepler's third law of planetary motion proved to be not approximately, but exactly, correct. For reasons that Kepler never knew but would have deeply appreciated, the sun's gravitational force and the planet's resistance to that force combine in such a way that any object orbiting the sun will have an orbital period whose square is proportional to the cube of the orbital semi-major axis.

In contrast to the mystical Kepler, his great Italian contemporary Galileo Galilei represented the prototype of the hard-nosed modern man, proud of his abilities, scornful of his rivals, not at all wrapped up in thoughts of the mystery of the cosmos. During the early years of the seventeenth century, while Kepler worked out the geometry of the solar system, Galileo made crucial discoveries that verified the sun-centered model. Not the inventor of the telescope but the first to use one for important astronomical observations, Galileo announced early in 1610 that Jupiter has four bright satellites, each of which orbits the planet in a different amount of time.

With this observation, the objections to the Copernican model based on a "dual motion" of the moon—an orbit around the Earth each month, while the Earth-moon system orbits the sun every year—disappeared, for if Jupiter's moons could perform such a duality, so too could our own moon. Later observations would show that Jupiter's four large moons, now called the Galilean satellites to honor the man who first saw them, obey their own version of Kepler's third law: The squares of their orbital periods vary in proportion to the cubes of their distances from Jupiter.

Galileo also saw that the moon's surface consists of mountainous regions and flat, broad plains, which he mistakenly named *maria,* meaning "seas" or "oceans" in Latin. The crucial result of this observation was to emphasize that the Earth might well resemble a celestial object—in this case, our moon—a world unto itself, also orbiting the sun and possessed of its own surface features. By provoking a series of disputes with Catholic theologians, Galileo nearly single-handedly brought the Copernican model into disrepute with all Catholic authorities, who called Galileo before theological tribunals and forced him, under threat of torture, to his famous abjuration of the model in which the Earth, not the sun, moves through the heavens (accompanied by Galileo's equally famous, though apocryphal, sotto voce abjuration of the abjuration). The authorities also forced him to live his declining years under house arrest, though famous travelers such as the English poet John Milton were free to visit Galileo in Florence. His death in 1642 preceded by just one year the birth of the man who would show why Kepler's laws are correct and Galileo was right after all— Isaac Newton.

Newton and the Mathematics of Planetary Motion

Newton was born several months after his father's death near Grantham, England, later famous as Margaret Thatcher's hometown. He showed early ability in mathematics, studied at Cambridge University, and spent a long and distinguished career as a professor there before moving on to still greater prominence as Master of the Mint. During a plague scare, when he was sent home like everyone else, Newton had his most fundamental insight: Everything in the universe attracts everything else with a force called gravitation. Not long after perceiving what we now call Newton's law of universal gravitation, Newton showed how this law, coupled with others that he elucidated, explains the motions of celestial objects. Though publication of his work on gravitation was delayed for decades, *Principia Mathematica Philosophiae Naturalis* (Mathematical Principles of Natural Philosophy) eventually became the most famous and influential work of science, rivaled only by Charles Darwin's *The Origin of Species.* By his mid-twenties, Newton had cracked the code of the physics of the cosmos.

Newton's greatest achievement was to conceive of a law of universal gravitation, a rule that would describe not simply the sun or the Earth or the satellites of Jupiter, but rather everything in the physical universe. In other words, Newton boldly generalized from a limited set of observations—the motions of the sun, moon, and planets, together with what he observed on Earth—to hypothesize a principle with universal application. The mathematics of this principle, though tremendously important, pale in significance in comparison with the concept that such a principle can and does exist.

Generations of students have learned how to recite Newton's rule for gravity, without pausing long to consider its implications. The universal law of gravitation

states that *every object with mass attracts every other object with mass, with an amount of force that varies in proportion to the product of the objects' masses, divided by the square of the distance between their centers.* Thus, for example, the Earth and moon attract each other with equal amounts of force: The Earth tries to pull the moon toward the Earth, while the moon exerts an equal amount of force on the Earth in the opposite direction. Similarly, the Earth attracts everyone on its surface with gravitational force, while each of us attracts the Earth with an amount of force exactly equal to the Earth's force on us.

Isaac Newton (1642–1727) realized that gravity can best be understood as a universal force that acts between all objects with mass.

Something must surely be wrong here. If we pull on the Earth as strongly as the Earth pulls on us, why do we feel the Earth's pull and the Earth seems to feel nothing? If the moon attracts the Earth as strongly as the Earth attracts the moon, why does the moon orbit the Earth, and not the reverse? Newton provided the answer to these questions with his most famous law of motion, which summarizes how objects behave with respect to forces exerted upon them. According to this rule, which has been verified by the most careful measurements possible, if a particular amount of force, **F**, acts on an object with a mass equal to **m**, that object will accelerate in the same direction as that net force. To accelerate means to change velocity, and the object will do so as long as the force acts on it. Newton's genius lay in seeing how the mass of the object, the amount of force applied to it, and the amount of the object's acceleration are interrelated. If we denote acceleration by **a**, Newton's law states that $a = F/m$. The same amount of force exerted on different objects produces *different* accelerations; in fact, the amount of acceleration from a particular force varies in *inverse* proportion to the object's mass.

Here Newton provides us with the explanation of why objects fall toward the Earth, and not the reverse, even though each object attracts the Earth with the same amount of force that the Earth exerts on it. Because the Earth has so much more mass than the falling objects, the same amount of force produces a much smaller acceleration on the Earth, which moves by an undetectable amount in response to the same amount of force that makes small objects accelerate rapidly downward.

Newton's rule, $a = F/m$, also explains why the moon orbits the Earth. Because the moon has only 1/81 of the Earth's mass, the same amount of force makes the moon accelerate 81 times more than

The moon attracts the Earth with the same amount of gravitational force as the Earth attracts the moon, but this force produces much less acceleration on the Earth, because it is far more massive than the moon.

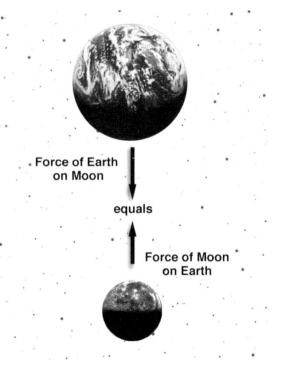

Force of Earth
on Moon

equals

Force of Moon
on Earth

the Earth. Both the Earth and the moon accelerate, and both move in orbit. (Their acceleration consists of constant changes in their directions of motion, rather than in the speeds with which they are moving.) The Earth and moon both orbit the center of mass of the Earth-moon system, which lies along the line joining the Earth and moon, but is 81 times farther from the moon's center than from the Earth's center. This puts the center of mass inside the Earth, though not at its center. The modest orbit that the Earth performs around the center of mass each month must be taken into account by astronomers, but pales to insignificance in comparison with the moon's motion in an orbit 81 times larger.

Using his law of gravitation and the rules of motion he had discovered, Newton analyzed what would happen if a more massive and less massive object attract each other by gravitation. He concluded that both objects will move in elliptical orbits around their common center of mass, with the less massive object performing a pro-portionately larger orbit. In fact, Newton showed that all of Kepler's laws of plane-tary motion—the elliptical orbits, the equal-areas-in-equal-times rule, and the rela-tionship between the orbits' sizes and periods—follow mathematically from the laws of motion and gravity that he (Newton) had perceived. Newton thus brilliantly melded the human capacity to create and to analyze mental models with our abilities to observe our surroundings carefully. The comparison of observations with the pre-dictions of our mental constructs has proven immensely useful to our understanding of the world around us; indeed, most scientists would say that this is the essence of scientific thinking.

Newton died in 1727, rich in honors and convinced that his research into biblical apocrypha would prove more important than his discoveries in astronomy and physics. His demonstration that his laws imply the results that Kepler had described put the seal of approval on the Copernican revolution. The two and a half centuries from Copernicus's birth to Newton's death saw immense changes in western Europe, none of which has had a longer-lasting impact than the new ways to regard the cos-

mos that sprang from Copernicus, Tycho, Kepler, Galileo, and Newton. From
Copernicus's contemporary Michelangelo, past Shakespeare who lived at the same
time as Galileo and Kepler, to the younger contemporaries of Newton such as John
Locke, whose theories of personal autonomy would strongly influence Thomas
Jefferson, we can trace the interrelation between a new view of the heavens and a
corresponding new view of man's role on Earth. Newton's life span well marks
European society's final transition from a worldview in which science struggled to
compete with received, theological wisdom into one where science could triumphant-
ly explain the basic motions in the solar system, and where everyone who fancied
himself educated had to know the fundamentals of Newton's work. How far have we
fallen since then!

Newton's insight received additional vindication half a century after his death,
when William Herschel discovered the sun's seventh planet, Uranus, and showed that
it obeys Kepler's and Newton's laws. In 1801, astronomers discovered the largest
asteroid, Ceres, moving between the orbits of Mars and Jupiter in excellent accord
with those laws. Three more asteroids, likewise moving as Newton said they should,
followed within a few years. An even greater success for Newton's work arose in
1846, after further observations of Uranus had revealed deviations from the orbit predicted on the basis of Newtonian knowledge. Sure that Newton was right, John
Couch Adams in England and Urbain Leverrier in France assumed that an object
beyond Uranus must be perturbing it with gravitational force, and independently
calculated the location of this object, which was promptly discovered by Johann Galle
in Berlin and named Neptune.

The ninth planet, Pluto, remains the only one found during the twentieth century,
and now appears more than a bit of a fluke. Like Uranus, Neptune seemed to show
deviations from the orbit predicted in the absence of a more distant planet to per-
turb it with gravitational force. This led to a detailed survey of the region of the sky
in which the hypothetical planet lay, and this search indeed revealed the planet Pluto

in 1930. However, later measurements of Pluto's size and mass, which turned out to be less than the moon's, demonstrated beyond doubt that Pluto could never make Neptune deviate significantly from the orbit it would have if Pluto did not exist. Apparently the observations of Neptune's motions had small errors; if so, the discovery of Pluto, though motivated by the belief that it was perturbing Neptune, was entirely fortuitous.

With astronomical history well under our belts, let us pick up the thread of cosmic history by turning from the last few centuries to the deep past, from the discovery of the solar system to our modern understanding of how the sun and its followers ever came to have their current properties.

THE FORMATION OF THE SOLAR SYSTEM

Astronomers now think that they understand the broad outlines of how the solar system formed. Of course, they have said that before, and were totally wrong. Fifty years ago, the best explanation seemed to be that a passing star's gravitational force extracted material from the sun that became the planets and their moons. Because close encounters between stars occur only rarely, this hypothesis implied that the solar system must be nearly unique in the Milky Way. Today, however, no astronomer believes in this theory, because calculations have shown that any hot gas pulled from the sun would soon evaporate into interstellar space rather than condense into planets.

Instead, the favored explanation envisions that the entire solar system formed from a single, pancakelike cloud of gas and dust, so that the sun and its retinue all have the same age, about 4.6 billion years. This hypothesis makes the formation of planetary systems an entirely mundane proposition, because astronomers consider our sun to be an entirely representative star, and believe that its formation process duplicated what has occurred billions of times in our galaxy. Even though astronomers still lack a definitive answer to the crucial question of what caused the process to begin nearly 5 billion years ago, and even though they have only a sketchy understanding of the early stages in the formation process, they feel that their understanding has improved greatly during the past few decades, and should continue to improve as we gather further clues to the story of our origins. An excursion through those clues proves surprisingly brief and equally provoking.

What evidence speaks to us from the long-vanished epochs when the Earth began? Astronomers have uncovered two types of facts, those that deal with what solar-system objects are made of, and those that describe how those objects orbit the sun. In both data sets, we can find highly significant patterns that appear to reflect the birth of the solar system. Deciphering these patterns can tell us about the processes that turned interstellar gas and dust into a star and a variegated conglomeration of attendants in orbit around it.

The Age of the Solar System

In theory, a determination of the age of the solar system can proceed by deriving the ages of each of the objects within it. These individual ages can be determined, at least to a minimum value, by obtaining a wide range of samples from each object, assigning a date of origin to each sample through techniques that rely on the slow and steady decay of the radioactive isotopes they contain, and then finding the greatest ages for each object's samples. For example, the oldest rocks on Earth have an age of 4.2 billion years, persuasive evidence that our planet itself must have at least this age. Furthermore, we know that plate-tectonic motions of the Earth's crust, familiarly called continental drift, have slowly buried rock layers beneath one another. This slow slippage of the Earth's crustal plates has buried nearly all of the oldest crust. As a result, finding truly ancient rocks, those more than one or two billion years old, requires immense effort; the world's-record rocks come from a few places in Greenland where the 4-billion-year-old crust somehow escaped burial.

This bodes ill for our project to collect ancient rocks from other planets and their moons—at least for those objects where plate-tectonic motions also occur. In the case of the four giant planets, where thousands of miles of gaseous outer layers envelop the solid cores, we may abandon hope of finding ancient rocks completely, at least for the foreseeable future. To put things charitably, our plan to date the solar system by examining rocks from all types of objects has barely begun. And yet we now have three additional pieces of significant information, two of them from objects that have fallen to Earth and one from our efforts in exploring our closest celestial neighbor.

To take the last one first, we have brought back to Earth a few hundred pounds of rocks from the moon. Because the moon is much smaller than the Earth, it lacks sufficient internal heat to drive plate-tectonic motions. As a result, geologists expected that the lunar surface should be covered with ancient rocks, and they found their predictions verified nearly three decades ago, when the first lunar samples came to Earth. The oldest moon rocks have ages of nearly 4.4 billion years, well beyond the ages of the oldest Earth rocks, and rank as the oldest rocks from any sizable object in the solar system.

To be sure, that competition has barely begun. Only one other object has furnished us with an ancient rock—the planet Mars. Twelve meteorites found on Earth have been identified as Martian in origin by the fact that their compositions differ

ALH 84001, a meteorite that fell to Earth from Mars, has an age of 4.3 billion years.

from those of Earth rocks but precisely match what the Viking spacecraft measured on Mars in 1976. Just one of those rocks, the famous Martian meteorite ALH 84001, has an age of 4.3 billion years, direct evidence that Mars, like Earth and the moon, formed well over 4 billion years ago.

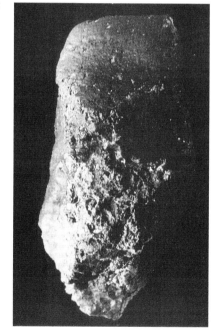

Other meteorites, not from any planet but simply debris with which the Earth has collided, provide the most comprehensive data on the age of the solar system. Most meteorites have enormous ages, and one class of them, the carbonaceous chondrites, consists entirely of ancient rocks. Meteorite experts believe that these objects, whose name reflects the fact that they are rich in carbon and contain glass inclusions called chondrules, are the most primitive pieces of matter yet examined in Earth-bound laboratories. Their ages cluster around 4.5 billion years, with the oldest dated to 4.55 billion. Many astronomers take this to mark a time close to the actual age of the solar system—the time when rocks first formed within the rotating disk of matter.

Thus all the age-related data fit together, perhaps because the data are so sparse. The hypothesis that all the planets, as well as the sun, formed at a time shortly before 4.55 billion years ago rests on the modest evidence from Earth, Mars, the moon, and meteorites. Within a decade or so, we should be able to sample pieces of asteroids and comets and to determine their ages. Since the experts confidently predict that we shall find ages close to 4.5 billion years, we can rate their performance, before long, by the newspaper stories about our ongoing exploration of the solar system. Before this happens, however, we ought to consider the evidence that tells us not when but how the solar system formed.

Orbital Regularities

Even a cursory glance at the eight largest objects that orbit the sun reveals a striking regularity: Four rocky planets—Mercury, Venus, Earth, and Mars—orbit relatively close to the sun, while four giant planets—Jupiter, Saturn, Uranus, and Neptune—circle our star at distances about 10 times greater than those of the inner planets. (We are dropping Pluto from immediate consideration because it more closely resembles a giant comet than a true planet.) *All eight planets orbit the sun in the same direction and in nearly the same plane.* This single fact speaks volumes in favor of the formation of the planets as condensations within a rotating disk of matter. Had the planets formed in some other manner, we would have no good reason why their orbital geometry should be so uniform. Of all the conjectures astronomers make about the formation process, the hypothesis that the solar system began within a single rotating disk seems to rest on the firmest evidence.

Five planets—Earth and the four giants—have significant satellite systems. Seven of their moons (our Earth's, the four "Galilean satellites" of Jupiter, and one each of Saturn's and Neptune's) are larger and more massive than Pluto. The worlds in orbit around the giant planets, and in particular Jupiter's four large Galilean satellites, mimic the solar system, as the moons all orbit in the same direction and in nearly the same plane. The conclusion follows (once we adopt the major premise for the formation of the solar system) that the giant planets formed at the centers of miniature disks of matter, with similar orbits for the worlds that condensed within those disks.

The less massive debris in the solar system—comets, asteroids, meteoroids, and cometlike objects that orbit the sun at distances beyond Pluto's—have so little mass that we commit only a small error in ignoring them when we describe the basic distribution and motion of matter in the solar system. Astronomers can, however, use the locations and orbits of these pieces of debris as crucial evidence in deducing the formation process. By combining the orbital data for the massive objects with the tracers provided by the less massive ones, astronomers have derived what we may now consider to be a standard model for the formation of the solar system. If this model successfully passes further testing, to be provided by the analysis of comets and other primordial pieces of the solar system, we shall gain additional confidence that astronomers finally have things right, after several centuries of missteps in explaining where the sun and its planets came from.

One additional, important clue to the formation of the solar system rests in the spacings between the planets' orbits. Unfortunately, this evidence, which fascinated Johann Kepler four centuries ago, remains as nearly indecipherable to us as it did to Kepler, despite the fact that modern astronomers know of three more planets than Kepler did.

The interval between successive planets' orbits tends to double as we look outward from the sun. This rule, often called the Bode-Titius law after the two astronomers who first noticed it, has its problems. It works only if we remove the innermost and outermost planets, Mercury and Pluto, from the list, and if we include the asteroids collectively as a "planet" whose distance equals the average distance from the asteroids to the sun. If we measure distances in units of the average Earth-sun distance, this approach produces seven gaps, whose sizes run as follows:

0.3   0.5   1.3   2.4   4.3   9.6   11

Only the last of these interplanetary spacings deviates significantly from the Bode-Titius rule. If we were to eliminate Neptune from the list of planets and to keep Pluto—hardly justifiable in view of the fact that Neptune has several thousand times Pluto's mass—the last entry would change from 11 to 20, and the Bode-Titius law would "work" much better. Honesty, however, compels the admission that the gaps

listed above are the ones on which the Bode-Titius rule of successive doublings must stand or fall as an accurate description of the solar system. For the time being, we must reserve judgment on what the rule tells us about the formation of our planetary system; some day, when we have found and measured

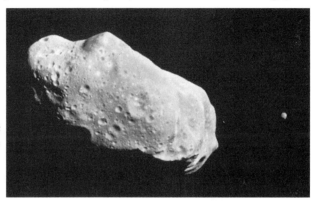

When the Galileo space-craft photo-graphed the asteroid called Ida (left), it found a small satellite asteroid, named Dactyl (right).

planetary systems around other stars, we shall see whether they too obey something like the Bode-Titius rule. If they do, astronomers will surely work overtime to show how the processes that form a planetary system impose a gap-doubling rule on the planets that orbit their parent stars.

The Standard Model for the Formation of the Solar System

During the past few decades, planetary scientists have incorporated the evidence we have summarized above into a now standard model to describe the formation of the solar system. That model includes the following scenario:

1. The entire solar system—sun, planets, satellites, comets, meteoroids, asteroids, and other debris—formed within part of a typical interstellar cloud, made of gas and dust, originally at an extremely low density. For reasons little known today, perhaps as the result of perturbations from a nearby star, a subclump within this cloud began to contract. This contraction began slowly and proceeded more rapidly as the sub-

clump shrank, because the gravitational forces among all parts of the clump increased in strength as the clump grew smaller.

2. The subclump that would produce the solar system formed a rotating disk of material, densest at its center. Such a disk was the natural result of the subclump's gravitationally induced contraction, provided that the subclump had some slow rotation to begin with. In that case, the rate of rotation would increase as the clump contracted, just as a high diver rotates more rapidly when she contracts her body. The flattening of the subclump arose from the fact that contraction could proceed more rapidly in directions parallel to the axis of spin than in the perpendicular directions.

In the standard model for the formation of the solar system, a rotating, roughly spherical cloud of gas and dust grew flatter as it contracted under its self-gravitational force. The rotating disk then produced clumps of matter, which accumulated enough material from the disk to become planets.

Rotating cloud of gas and dust . . .

... flattens as it contracts.

Planetesimals form within the rotating disk ...

... forming planets that orbit the central star.

3. Calculations imply that the formation process occurred quite rapidly, on an astronomical view of things, consuming no more than tens of millions of years and perhaps only millions of years for the crucial stages in which large objects assembled themselves from smaller ones.

4. Within the rotating disk, the central condensation became the sun, while subclumps, formed from rings of material at different distances from the center, became the planets and their satellite systems. The reasons that these subclumps formed,

with orbital spacings summarized by the Bode-Titius law, remain largely if not wholly unknown to this day. Our best hope for understanding the process in any detail probably lies with hopes of observing planetary systems not only after they have formed, as in the case of our own solar system, but also as they form. We can hope to achieve this goal once we have telescopes and interferometer systems capable of finding planets and planet-forming disks around nearby stars.

Comets: The Proof of the Standard Model

A crass reaction to the sketch presented above might be: Until you can show me those different stages you have imagined, I have little if any reason to believe what you tell me about the formation of the sun, planets, moons, and asteroids. In order to avoid this harsh reaction, let us take a moment to clarify the evidence in favor of the standard model described above. Our clarification consists of linking our knowledge of how objects interact gravitationally to the observed facts about the solar system, and of concentrating on a portion of the solar system heretofore neglected in this chapter, the comets.

Insofar as astronomers' ability to observe them goes, comets labor under a tremendous handicap, what scientists call a selection effect. Even with our most modern equipment, we can detect comets only when they come close to the sun. In this context, "close" means roughly "inside the orbit of Jupiter," that is, within about five times the Earth's distance from the sun. At greater distances, comets remain invisible, because they are essentially city-size dirty snowballs, small objects that reflect light poorly, bits of cosmic debris far smaller than planets or even their medium-size moons. When a comet nears the sun, the solar heating loosens the comet's outermost layer, allowing that material to fuzz out and to be pushed away from the comet by the pressure from sunlight and by particles ejected from the sun. This newly released material reflects light with high efficiency: Instead of being locked inside the comet by the billions, every individual atom and molecule now has a chance to intercept sunlight and direct some of it our way. The comet grows a fuzzy "coma" and a long, highly rarefied "tail," which last no longer than it takes the comet to round the sun and once again to reach a distance comparable to Jupiter's from the source of the cometary vaporization and reflected light.

From the few thousand comets that astronomers have discovered, they conclude that the sun's family of comets totals about—one trillion! This bold extrapolation derives from astronomers' knowledge of the difficulties that comets face in attaining proximity to the sun, the regions where we may see them. To reach this proximity, a typical comet, moving in an immense orbit that never carries it even inside the orbit of Pluto, must somehow be diverted—probably by a close encounter with another comet—into an orbit that approaches the sun within a much smaller distance than before. Second, on its first trip toward the inner parts of the solar system, the comet must avoid the gravitational effects from the four giant planets, which tend to fling the comet back out into the depths of interstellar space. Only if the comet leaps both hurdles (metaphorically) can it penetrate the inner sanctum, approaching the sun sufficiently closely for its coma and tail to render it visible to astronomers on Earth.

The Oort Cloud and the Kuiper Belt

From their few thousand comet sightings, astronomers have concluded that most of the sun's comets orbit the sun at distances many thousand times the Earth's distance. Collectively, these comets form the Oort cloud, named after the Dutch astronomer Jan Oort (pronounced as either OOhrt or OARt). The Oort cloud of comets forms a sphere centered on the sun, reaching halfway to the closest stars, and contains perhaps a trillion member comets. All of these comets are ancient assemblages of ice, rock, and dust—dirty snowballs nearly 5 billion years old.

A simple explanation of the Oort cloud would conclude that all these trillion comets must have formed in this spherical array, and that the solar-system-information then somehow changed from a spherical distribution to one as flat as a pancake. As a result of this flattening, the planets assembled themselves only a hundred million years or so later within this pancake.

Indeed this sort of interpretation once found favor among some groups of astronomers, only to be totally rejected today, partly because it is not clear why comets should ever form in the depths of interstellar space, and partly because this interpretation ignores the dynamical interplay that has occurred between the comets and the two most massive planets, Jupiter and Saturn. To conclude that the comets in the Oort cloud assembled themselves at distances thousands of times the Earth-sun distance, astronomers require some mechanism that explains how cometary objects can form from immensely rarefied gas and dust. Because they have no such mechanism, astronomers now conclude that comets formed at more modest distances, only a few hundred times the Earth's distance from the sun. Their modern interpretation of the Oort cloud assigns its spherical shape not to a spherical cloud of gas and dust that made the solar system, but to the random flinging of comets into the outer depths of the solar system by their close encounters with Jupiter and Saturn. In other words, although comets themselves formed before the planets did, the Oort cloud of comets took shape only after the planets had formed. Where, then, were the comets before the gravitational forces from Jupiter and Saturn sent them into the Oort cloud?

The name of the answer to this question echoes that of another famous Dutch astronomer, Gerard Kuiper, who spent many fruitful years as professor in Chicago and Tucson and whose name rhymes with a word halfway between KOY-per and KYE-per. The Kuiper belt of comets falls short of the tremendous population of the Oort cloud, though it can claim millions of comets (whose existence astronomers have deduced, as they have those in the Oort cloud, from relatively few actual sightings). As its name vaguely implies, the Kuiper belt has a flattened shape and represents the extension of the plane that contains the orbits of the large planets. In terms of the history of the solar system, however, we ran time backward in the previous sentence. First came the Kuiper belt, and then the planets formed: They and their satellites, plus the asteroids and meteoroids, were made from the inner regions of the pancake of matter that still girdles the sun.

The Big Picture of How the Solar System Formed

Picture, then, the solar-system-in-formation nearly 5 billion years ago. Within a cloud of interstellar gas and dust, a subclump has formed and contracted under its self-gravitation. Because this subclump had some rotation (though astronomers lack any detailed understanding of what processes would make this so), the rate of rotation increased as the cloud contracted, a reflection of the rule of physics called the conservation of angular momentum. The increased rate of rotation caused the subclump to grow flatter, until its vertical thickness was less than one one-hundredth of its extent in the directions perpendicular to its axis of rotation. This pancakelike flattening helped to concentrate matter, so that within the subclump that became the solar system, billions upon billions of much smaller bits of matter coagulated, comets aborning around the huge central concentration that became the sun.

Within a hundred million years or less, the flattened subclump became a star surrounded by a gaseous, dusty disk of matter, within which immense numbers of ice-and-rock comets orbited the newborn sun at distances ranging from a modest fraction of an astronomical unit up to several hundred times the Earth-sun distance. Even before the sun became a nuclear-fusing star, it emitted heat as the result of its gravitationally induced contraction. This heat had significant effects on the inner regions of the Kuiper belt, driving the gas into interstellar space. When we think of this key hundred million years—roughly from 4.65 to 4.55 billion years ago—we must picture a competition between gravitation and evaporation. Just as cometlike objects formed and some of them began to aggregate themselves into planets—planets sufficiently massive to retain gas by their gravitational forces—the heat from the protosun

(sun-in-formation) was evaporating the reservoir of gas in the Kuiper belt.

The inner planets lost their battle to retain gas, while the giant planets won theirs, simply because they formed at much greater distances from the sun. What counts in this struggle was the mass that a planet attained while the gas was escaping, compared with the rate at which the gas escaped into the depths of space, driven by the heat from the sun as it formed. If we took Jupiter now and brought it to the Earth's distance from the sun, it could still retain most of its hydrogen and helium, even though it would grow much hotter. But we never had a Jupiter-mass planet in our vicinity, because while the Earth was, so to speak, attempting to grow a Jupiter, the gas managed to escape. Therefore we must rest content with our planet's mass, suppressing our envy of Jupiter's more than three-hundredfold superiority, the result of its retention of much of the hydrogen and helium in its region of the Kuiper belt.

With the big picture well in hand, we can turn to a survey of the results of the formation process, working our way from the sun's innermost planet, Mercury, outward to the vast dimensions of the Oort cloud of comets. Come along for the ride, and take a look at what we know about the solar system. After all, your tax dollars brought us most of this knowledge, just as they continue to fund the discoveries of the new millennium.

MERCURY AND VENUS

Thirty years ago, no one had seen the surfaces of either Mercury or Venus. In those days of my youth, astronomers knew so little about Mercury, the innermost as well as the smallest of the sun's true planets (so long as we deny Pluto that title) that they were still arguing about its period of rotation, while Venus, totally enshrouded in its gauzy, opaque atmosphere, maintained a maidenly refusal to yield its secrets to human examination. All this changed dramatically during the early 1970s, as automated spacecraft revealed fundamental facts about Mercury and Venus.

Mercury

Mercury had remained an enigma to astronomers because of its small size and the fact that the planet always appears close to the sun, which makes it difficult to observe with even the finest telescopes. Because Mercury moves so rapidly in orbit, and therefore changes its position quite noticeably from one night to the next, ancient cultures named the planet after the swift messenger of the gods. As their observations became more accurate, astronomers saw that Mercury has the most elongated orbit of any of the sun's eight "true" planets, an orbit that carries the planet out to distances 20 percent greater, and in to distances 20 percent less, than Mercury's average distance from the sun, which equals 39 percent of the average Earth-sun distance. Mercury's diameter, only 38 percent of the Earth's, gives it a volume just under 6 percent of our planet's, or about three times the volume contained in our own moon.

During the first half of this century, keen-eyed observers claimed to have discerned blotchy surface features on Mercury; they used their observations to deduce that Mercury rotates once in 88 days, the same time that it takes to orbit the sun. Radar observations from Earth eventually showed that these observers had been mistaken: Mercury rotates once every 58 2/3 days, exactly two-thirds of its 88-day orbital period. This correspondence makes the same part of Mercury face the sun every second time the planet comes closest to the sun in its elliptical orbit. The distribution of matter inside Mercury must have an asymmetry that makes the planet denser in some directions outward from its center than in others. The sun's gravitational force has locked onto these denser regions, and has slowly changed Mercury's rotational period so that the denser regions face the sun during every other close approach. This gravitational locking between an object's rotational and orbital periods appears in many places throughout the solar system, but it typically does so in the simplest possible manner, in which the locking has become perfect. This type of perfection appears in the locking of the moon's rotation, which occurs with exactly the same 27 1/3-day period that the moon takes to orbit once around the Earth. Mercury, in contrast, rotates in a "3-to-2 resonance": The planet performs three rotations during every two orbits around the sun.

Because Mercury rotates only slowly, the sunward-facing side of Mercury heats to a temperature of nearly 700 degrees Fahrenheit, hot enough to melt soft metals, while the opposite side of the planet cools to 350 degrees below zero Fahrenheit, colder than any other place in the inner solar system. During a complete day-and-night cycle on Mercury, which spans 176 days, the rocks on the surface therefore pass through temperature changes that span about 1,000 degrees Fahrenheit. Any explorers on Mercury would face enormous problems in alternately heating and cooling themselves—problems that could be avoided by landing at one of Mercury's poles, where the temperature remains between the readings on the frighteningly hot day side and the amazingly cold night side.

Though a small planet, Mercury is remarkably dense—unexpectedly so because more massive objects produce greater self-gravitational forces, which squeeze their interiors to higher densities. With a mass just over 5 percent of the Earth's, Mercury's ratio of mass to volume gives the planet an average density of 5.4 grams per cubic centimeter, noticeably greater than the densities of either Venus or Mars, which are significantly larger than Mercury. Mercury's density almost equals that of Earth, the largest of the four inner planets, which most effectively squeezes its innards through gravitational forces to produce a high density of matter. Astronomers' best explanation for Mercury's high density envisions a giant impact that blew much of the planet's lighter material into space soon after the planets had formed and while they were still being bombarded by the raw material that made them. Though this theory appears reasonable, direct evidence of such a nearly cataclysmic impact is lack-

Mariner 10 photographed the planet Mercury in 1974.

ing, perhaps to be uncovered one day when spacecraft land on the Mercurian surface.

For now, we must make do with the results from a single spacecraft mission, NASA's Mariner 10, which made three close flybys of Mercury in 1974 and 1975 and sent to Earth almost all the information we now have about the planet's surface features. Mariner 10's successful operation furnished astronomers with a range of information approximately equal to what was known of our moon before the space era began. And as is true for the moon, which keeps one hemisphere hidden from our view, Mercury showed only one hemisphere to Mariner 10, whose images have resolution equal to the best photographs of the moon made from the Earth's surface.

Those photographs show that despite the extreme temperature changes on Mercury, which will eventually cause the planet's surface features to crack and erode, Mercury's surface still has sharp topographic relief, highly reminiscent of the lunar landscape. Indeed, a casual glance at a Mariner 10 photograph of Mercury would leave most of us believing that we had seen a picture of our moon. A host of craters crowd the image, with plains of frozen lava reminiscent of those on the moon; these plains presumably formed in the same way on both objects, as the result of lava flows that occurred after the largest impacts. The largest of these impact flows, the Caloris basin, has the size of Texas. The large number of impact craters strongly suggest that we are seeing remnants from the era of intense bombardment in the early solar system, estimated to have lasted from about 4.5 billion to 3.9 billion years ago.

During the past decade, radio waves sent from Earth to bounce off Mercury have revealed a totally unexpected phenomenon about the polar caps that might someday provide a refuge to Mercurian explorers. The details of how the polar regions reflect radio waves show that they contain volatile (easily evaporating) molecular compounds frozen underneath the polar surfaces. Since the most likely such volatile compound is ordinary ice, this discovery implies that regions not far below the poles of Mercury have temperatures roughly comparable to those in the polar regions of Earth and Mars. Although we can easily imagine that these temperatures might exist on Mercury, astronomers have difficulty in imagining how water ever reached the poles of Mercury in the first place. The recent discovery of ice beneath the poles of our moon, described in the next chapter, poses a similar problem, which may turn out to have a similar solution.

Venus, the Near-Twin of Earth

Venus, brightest and closest of the planets that appear in our skies, has been veiled in mystery throughout most of humanity's efforts to understand the solar system. Visible, like all the planets, only by the sunlight it reflects, Venus glows with a creamy yellow tint, which reminded ancient cultures of feminine beauty, and seemed quite different from Mars's bloodlike hue. When Galileo turned his telescope on the planet, he saw that Venus exhibits a sequence of phases analogous to the moon's, because as Venus and Earth move along their orbits, we see a changing fraction of the sunlit half of Venus. As it moves in a nearly circular orbit around the sun at 72 percent of the Earth-sun distance, Venus on occasion approaches Earth within a mere 25 million miles, the closest approach of any planet. At those times, however, Venus does not appear at its brightest, because we see only mostly the dark side of Venus and only a thin crescent of the sunlit side.

Neither Galileo nor any other observer on Earth could ever see the surface of Venus. Unlike Earth, where the cloud cover often parts to reveal the land and oceans below, Venus has an atmosphere that forever shrouds its surface from view. Even so, astronomers could deduce the planet's diameter (96 percent of Earth's) and mass (81.5 percent of Earth's), which make Venus the planet most like the Earth in size and mass. On rare occasions, Venus passes directly between the Earth and the sun, producing a "transit of Venus," when the planet appears as a small black dot moving across the solar disk. Transits of Venus typically occur only at intervals of more than a century, but then we get a twofer: two transits within eight years. The next two transits are right around the corner, in the years 2004 and 2012. The transits of Venus first revealed the planet's thick atmosphere, which gives a diffuse edge to the visible disk as Venus crosses in front of the sun; this contrasts with the hard edge that airless Mercury shows during its transits. Venus's atmosphere reflects light more efficiently than our Earth's, and dominates the situation on Venus's surface; indeed, the atmosphere has turned Venus into an unbearable hell (by Earthly standards)—a hell that we might yet bring accidentally to our own planet.

What is this stifling blanket that makes Venus so unpleasant? After astronomers had developed spectroscopic techniques to analyze the sunlight reflected by a planet, they proceeded to discover certain fascinating and significant details about Venus's atmosphere. On the fascinating side, Venus's high reflectivity arises from droplets of sulfuric acid high in its atmosphere: The planet's lovely, yellow-white appearance comes from the presence of what we regard as a lethal gas! Sulfuric acid can be created in a planet's atmosphere when sunlight induces chemical reactions between hydrogen and sulfur dioxide molecules. The sulfur dioxide typically emerges from volcanoes, so the clouds of Venus provide good evidence that numerous volcanic eruptions have occurred on Venus's surface.

Even more significant is the fact that Venus's atmosphere contains enormous amounts of carbon dioxide—more than 10,000 times the amount of carbon dioxide in the atmosphere of Earth. Since carbon dioxide forms a bit less than one percent of our atmosphere, Venus has an atmosphere roughly 100 times thicker than our planet's. All types of molecules other than carbon dioxide, such as the sulfuric acid in the clouds, form only a tiny part of Venus's atmospheric shroud. Carbon dioxide, the dominant atmospheric component, creates the inferno we call Venus.

Carbon Dioxide and the Greenhouse Effect

Since Venus orbits the sun at only 72 percent of the Earth-sun distance, we would expect the planet to be hotter than Earth, though not so hot as Mercury. But during the 1950s, as astronomers made improved observations of the infrared and radio waves emitted by Venus, they found a temperature close to 900 degrees Fahrenheit, much hotter than Mercury, by far the hottest surface in the solar system (not counting the sun's 10,000 degrees, of course).

A long debate followed as to whether this high temperature actually existed on Venus rather than in its ionosphere, the region high in Venus's atmosphere where solar radiation strips the electrons from atoms, providing an excellent layer for reflecting radio waves. The late Carl Sagan argued for what turned out to be correct despite its apparent near impossibility: Venus maintains its surface temperature more than 600 degrees Fahrenheit hotter than Earth's. Sagan also perceived the correct explanation for this startling planetary feat. Citing a phenomenon that has gained prominence on Earth during the four decades since he first wrote on the subject, Sagan called attention to the powerful influence that carbon dioxide can exert on a planet's atmosphere and surface.

In modest amounts, carbon dioxide (CO_2) provides a nearly transparent gas, quite harmless to humans and other animals and essential to terrestrial plants. The transparency of carbon dioxide, however, refers only to the transmission of what we call visible light, electromagnetic radiation with wavelengths between 380 and 750 nanometers. Earth's atmosphere allows solar radiation whose wavelengths lie in this range to pass unhindered, while blocking most radiation with longer or shorter wavelengths. As a result, human eyes (and the eyes of most other Earth creatures) have evolved to detect visible light, not ultraviolet radiation, with shorter wavelengths, nor infrared radiation, whose wavelengths are longer than those of visible light. If we had "infrared eyes," capable of registering incoming infrared radiation, we would have noticed that even a modest concentration of carbon-dioxide gas hinders the transmission of infrared, and large amounts block infrared completely.

An atmosphere made of carbon dioxide provides a planetary analog to a one-way mirror. Most of the sun's radiation will penetrate the atmosphere, because it consists mainly of radiation with ultraviolet and visible-light wavelengths. If the planet's surface reflected all incoming radiation without changing it, the atmosphere would allow the radiation to escape unhindered. But planetary surfaces are not perfect mirrors. Instead, the solar radiation striking a planet's surface carries energy that heats the surface, not to the thousands of degrees that typify the outer layers of stars like the sun, but to hundreds of degrees on the absolute scale—somewhere between minus 400 and plus 900 degrees Fahrenheit, depending on the distance from the star to the planet. At these temperatures, the surfaces radiate energy in the form of infrared radiation, to which a carbon-dioxide atmosphere forms an opaque shield. Instead of escaping into space, the infrared radiation strikes one of the carbon-dioxide molecules in the atmosphere and gives its energy to the molecule, exciting the molecule, as physicists say, into a higher-energy state.

This means that the atmosphere grows hotter from the energy deposited by the infrared radiation that it absorbs. The heating causes the atmospheric molecules to radiate infrared, some of which heads downward and warms the ground still further, while the remainder meets other carbon-dioxide molecules in the atmosphere and is absorbed in its turn. After undergoing a large amount of absorption and re-radiation, some infrared radiation does in fact leak from the top of the planet's atmosphere, but it does so only after the repeated processes of absorption and radiation have warmed the entire atmosphere and the surface of the planet. This creates a "greenhouse effect" analogous to the trapping of heat by a garden greenhouse.

Among the sun's planets, Venus has a killer greenhouse effect. Thanks to the enormous amounts of carbon dioxide in its atmosphere, Venus has a surface that bakes at temperatures well above 800 degrees Fahrenheit, nearly hot enough to melt the rocks! Without this atmosphere, Venus's surface temperature would be more than 700 degrees less, not so far above the average temperature on Earth. Our planet's atmosphere likewise provides a greenhouse effect, both from its carbon dioxide and also from its variable water-vapor content. Water molecules, though not so efficient as carbon dioxide in absorbing infrared radiation, is not half bad at it; together with the Earth's carbon dioxide, it creates a greenhouse effect of 20 to 30 degrees Fahrenheit. Without an atmosphere, the mid-latitudes on Earth would have temperatures like those of the Arctic and Antarctic regions. With it, we have a climate just right for us, as well as oxygen to breathe. Note, however, that the primary constituents of Earth's atmosphere, nitrogen and oxygen molecules, provide essentially no greenhouse effect, for they do not absorb much infrared, in sharp contrast to water-vapor and carbon-dioxide molecules.

How is it that Venus has so much carbon dioxide in its atmosphere, while Earth has so little? The answer lies with life. Living creatures on Earth have effectively buried most of the carbon dioxide near our planet's surface, allowing us to elude the greenhouse-effect hound of fate that has raised hell on our neighbor planet. And how has this come to pass? Tiny creatures floating in the oceans continually use some of the carbon dioxide dissolved in seawater to make their shells. As these creatures die, these shells fall to the ocean floor, where many of them eventually form limestone rocks, rich in carbon and oxygen, of which the white cliffs of Dover provide a fine example. As this process continues, steadily removing carbon dioxide from the oceans, additional carbon dioxide dissolves from the atmosphere into the seas to replace it. The cycle of carbon-dioxide intake and replenishment closes as limestone rocks slowly wear away, releasing carbon dioxide into the air. The net effect of the cycle is to keep most of the carbon dioxide locked into rocks, with only a tiny fraction of the total residing in either the atmosphere or the oceans. If we were to grind up all the limestone rocks near the Earth's surface, we would release into the air about as much carbon dioxide as Venus has in its atmosphere—about 10,000 times more than we have now. Then we could be Venus, perhaps even more Venuslike than Venus is today.

If this project seems overly ambitious, consider the modest efforts now underway. Whenever humans burn fossil fuels to obtain heat and power, we increase the amount of carbon dioxide in the atmosphere of our life-giving planet, and thereby increase the amount of the atmospheric greenhouse effect. No one knows just how much the increased greenhouse effect will raise the Earth's temperature, and still less how the rise in temperature will affect life on Earth. What lies completely beyond question is that we have already embarked on a global experiment by significantly raising the average carbon-dioxide content of our planet's atmosphere. Meanwhile, take a good look at Venus if you want to see what a really powerful greenhouse effect can achieve.

Spacecraft Visits to Venus

A little more than forty years ago, humanity entered the space age by launching the first artificial satellites of Earth. Within the next three decades, automated space probes had flown past, or landed on, all of the sun's planets save Pluto. Of the two dozen major spacecraft sent to the Earth's planetary neighbors, nine have landed on the closest planet, Venus, where they spent only a few hours sending data back to Earth before succumbing to the intense heat.

These nine visitors were all Soviet-made: Venera 7 landed first, in 1970; Venera 8 arrived in 1972; Venera 9 and 10 followed in 1975; Venera 11 and 12 touched down in 1978; Venera 13 and 14 landed in 1982; and Venera 18 arrived in 1985. The first six apparently landed on old lava flows that showed few individual rocks, but Venera 13 reached a location with many small rocks and even fine-grained soil or ash. The nine Venera landers established that Venus's surface, though almost hot enough to melt rocks, does not do so: The lava remains solid, and so do the smaller rocks and grit.

Because Venus's thick atmosphere prevented these spacecraft from seeing more than a few yards in any direction, and because Venus's intense heat soon left them inoperable, the Venera mission uncovered little more than these bare facts. To do better—and to understand the planet as a whole—astronomers knew that they must rely on radar systems that can look through the opaque clouds.

In 1982, the Soviet spacecraft Venera 13 and Venera 14 obtained these two images of the surface of Venus.

Radar Reveals the Surface of Venus

Venus's tremendous heat has almost no effect on astronomers' other tool for examining what lies below the clouds of Venus. Radar systems, operating both from Earth and in orbit around Venus, can pierce its opaque veil of atmosphere, because the long-wavelength radiation they employ finds essentially no obstacle to penetration from the aerosol particles that eternally block all visible-light radiation. Well aware of this fact, astronomers have long placed high hopes on mapping the surface of Venus by bouncing radio waves from it. This radar (*ra*dio *d*etection *a*nd *r*anging) approach has paid handsome dividends in our quest to understand the surface of Venus. Radar echoes detected by the Arecibo Observatory in Puerto Rico first established Venus's period of rotation, and radar systems in orbit around Venus made the first maps of the planet's surface. These systems steadily improved in resolution, from a limit of about a mile for the smallest observable features, attained by the Soviet Venera 15 and Venera 16 spacecraft in 1983, to about 100 yards, achieved by the Pioneer Venus spacecraft that orbited from 1978 into 1980, and then to about 50 yards, with an advanced system for making radar images, carried by the Magellan spacecraft that studied Venus from 1990 through 1992.

The radar images of Venus's surface—and particularly those from the Magellan spacecraft—have led astronomers to revise their conception of the planet's geological history. We now know that Venus's geological activity both resembles the Earth's and differs from it. Venus has tectonic activity, as the Earth does, but it does not have the crustal plates whose motions characterize this activity on our planet. Like Earth, Venus has an interior divided into a crust (the outermost few miles of rock) and a somewhat denser mantle, which extends downward for thousands of miles and surrounds a far denser core. On Earth, the different crustal plates float atop the mantle, gliding on hot material, called magma, that is just at the melting point of its rocks. The plates slowly slide past one another, collide head-on, or slip over one another, producing most of our planet's earthquakes and volcanoes. Instead of this plate-tectonic activity, Venus has what some planetary scientists call "blob tectonics." Currents of hot rock (magma) must move slowly through Venus's mantle, just as they do on Earth, but those currents do not "float" crustal plates, either because Venus's currents are weaker than Earth's or because its crust is stronger. The magma can punch through Venus's crust to produce volcanoes and other isolated features, some-what similar to the "hot spot" beneath the Pacific plate on Earth that has produced the Hawaiian Islands by volcanic activity.

Venus further resembles our planet in possessing plateaus and mountain ranges, similar in height and extent to those we know on Earth. The most prominent plateaus on Venus are in the Lakshmi plain, about four miles higher than the rest of the planet's surface. Close to Lakshmi, the Maxwell Mountains rise more than six miles above the low plains of Venus. These altitudes closely match those for the Tibetan plateau and the nearby Himalayas in Asia. Just as those Earthly features arise from the collision of two crustal plates, the plateaus and mountains of Venus must owe their origin to some force that squeezes the planet's crust and makes it bulge. But if plate tectonics does not occur on our sister planet, what are those forces? The admission that astronomers have yet to answer this question underscores their desire to investigate Venus further with an array of automated spacecraft, still a gleam in the eyes of planetary scientists.

The plateaus are the exceptional features of Venus. Most of its surface, like Mercury's and the moon's, consists of frozen lava plains such as Lakshmi. Volcanic eruptions produced this lava, not recently but not so long ago in comparison with the 4.6 billion years since Venus formed. That relatively few craters dot the plains of Venus suggests an age of about half a billion years, only one-ninth or so of Venus's total life span. By calculating how much lava it takes to make a plain on Venus, astronomers conclude that the volcanoes on Venus produce new lava at roughly the same rate as volcanoes do on Earth's land surface. This is an average rate, however; from the erosion seen in the craters, astronomers also deduce that the rate of volcanism on Venus has varied widely. It is quite possible that most of the lava plains were made within just a few million years, half a billion or so years ago, and the planet has become much quieter—volcanically speaking—since that time.

Some of the volcanic "eruptions" on Venus must have been closer in spirit to slow, prolonged wheezes; they consisted of lava so viscous that we can hardly call them eruptions. These volcanic burps left behind round domes, rising a mile or so above the lava plains, with diameters of a few miles up to as many as 30 miles. Although Earth has some volcanic domes, they lack the noble symmetry of those on

Venus, a symmetry that apparently arose from the slow, steady efflux of viscous lava.

If treacly, tar-like lava seems more annoying than amusing, consider that Venus also has places where lava has flowed in long, thin rivers for hundreds, even thousands, of miles, far longer than any known lava flows on Earth, which are measured in the tens of miles at most. The lava that made the long, frozen rivers must have had properties opposite to those described as "viscous," for it managed to travel thousands of miles in a relatively short time, before cooling to the point that further

The Magellan spacecraft's radar systems revealed circular domes on Venus, each about 30 miles across and a mile high.

motion became impossible. If volcanic activity should resume on Venus, colonists could theoretically find themselves in danger of being swept away by lava from the other side of the planet.

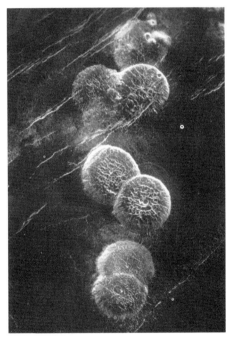

Venus does possess a series of tectonic features not found on any other object in the solar system. These features, called coronae, are rings of concentric circles that span several hundred miles, surrounding a low, raised dome, and typically crossed by a radial pattern of tracks that extend outward from the dome. The likeliest explanation for the coronae may be that plumes of hot magma, attempting to break through to the planet's crust, have either failed to do so, or have not yet done so, leaving only a corona to mark the spot where hot magma lies miles beneath the surface.

Let us bid farewell to Venus, mindful that there but for the oceans' grace goes our planet. It is time to consider the sun's third planet, our beloved Earth, happily occupying its Goldilocks-like position between Venus and Mars, not too hot nor too cold, but just right—for us.

CHAPTER FIVE

THE EARTH AND THE MOON

The Home Planet

We inhabit the sun's third planet, continuously orbiting our parent star, proud in knowledge that our ancestors would have regarded as assertions too odd to be taken seriously. Human intuition, formed in utter disregard of the higher learning of astronomy, tells us that we live on a stable platform beneath the rotating dome of heaven. Some of us may temporarily overcome this belief to recognize—logically!—that we inhabit a mote of dust in the vasty cosmic deep, but we never completely accept this logic, and must constantly guard against letting our intuition preside over our attempts to understand the cosmos. Astronomers themselves have fallen victim to such speculation again and again, successively assigning to Earth, to the sun, even to our Milky Way galaxy a pre-eminent role in the cosmos. Not all guesswork is wrong, but we must always strive to remain aware of the crucial astronomical fact regarding our intuition, that intuition operates without reference to realms beyond the Earth. Only by remembering this truism can we hope to reach a correct under-standing of the mighty universe that contains our planet.

On the other hand, blue-green Earth is such an extraordinary planet in our solar system that we may be excused for believing it to be a peculiar case in the cosmos. Earth is special, but not for its size, density, mass, or rotation, characteristics that it shares (in approximation) with one or more of the sun's three other inner planets. What makes Earth stand out among the planets are its atmosphere and—much more—its oceans. Earth's atmosphere and oceans allow life to flourish abundantly, though we have also found microscopic organisms on Earth that require neither of these to survive. Acting in conjunction with the geological processes that create vol-canoes, and with the movement of continental plates, the atmosphere and oceans have continuously changed the face of Earth, leaving our planet in a far different state today than it was during the early or middle stages of its 4.6-billion-year history. Though our neighboring planets, Mars and Venus, exhibit signs of ancient volcanoes and some geological activity, they have nothing like Earth's atmosphere or oceans. Not coincidentally, these planets also appear devoid of living creatures on their surfaces.

Having evolved to take full advantage of them, we humans find Earth's crust, oceans, and atmosphere quite normal and familiar. We would do well, however, to note that none of these remains in anything like its original state. Nature has changed them, and as we perform global experiments on the oceans or atmosphere, we risk finding out just what effects any significant changes in these integuments of Earth can have upon us. Let us celebrate Earth's planetary standing by tracing the history of the gaseous and watery fluids that envelop its surface.

The Veil of Air

Earth's atmosphere consists mainly of nitrogen (N_2) and oxygen (O_2) molecules, which, respectively, form about 78 and 21 percent of the air. The remaining small percentage consists of varying amounts of water vapor (H_2O), along with small numbers of argon atoms and still smaller amounts of carbon-dioxide molecules. When we compare Earth's atmosphere with those of our neighbor planets, Mars and Venus, a striking difference emerges: Those two planets have atmospheres made primarily of carbon dioxide, with few nitrogen and almost no oxygen molecules.

We now know that our atmospheric characteristics have arisen primarily from the presence of life on Earth. As we described in our tour of Venus, microscopic organisms floating in the oceans of Earth have caused most of the carbon dioxide near the Earth's surface to become locked into carbonate (carbon-oxygen) rocks, made with carbon dioxide from the atmosphere that had dissolved into seawater. Just as important (to us!), other single-celled sea creatures expelled oxygen into the Earth's atmosphere billions of years ago as a byproduct of their metabolic activities.

This pollution, the greatest our atmosphere has ever experienced, turned out to be useful for animals. Once the atmosphere had become rich in oxygen, animals could evolve to take advantage of it, combining oxygen with the food that they ate as a means of tapping the sources of energy stored in plants. Perhaps the pollution that we now spew into our planet's atmosphere may someday prove useful to new breeds of creatures capable of surviving long after we have passed on to our just desserts.

Because our atmosphere consists mainly of nitrogen and oxygen, which do not trap infrared radiation effectively, the Earth's atmospheric greenhouse effect provides only a pale copy of the mighty greenhouse on Venus, whose thick carbon-dioxide atmosphere raises the surface temperature by more than 700 degrees Fahrenheit. Earth's greenhouse effect arises from the small fraction of atmospheric gas that consists of carbon-dioxide or water-vapor molecules, both of which block the passage of infrared radiation and trap part of this energy close to the planet's surface. Modest though Earth's greenhouse may be by planetary standards, it makes a significant difference to life on Earth, since it raises our planet's surface temperature by about 30 degrees Fahrenheit. Without a greenhouse effect, life on Earth would have become either more tolerant of the cold or more concentrated in the Earth's warmer, equatorial regions.

As we mused from the depths of Venus's atmosphere, we perform an experiment fraught with serious risk as we continue to pour carbon dioxide into the air. Long before our planet fully resembles Venus, we could easily warm ourselves out of a good situation. The jury is still out on just how much of an additional greenhouse effect will arise from human additions to the carbon-dioxide budget, and on how severely this additional warming will affect life on Earth. Since each of us funds this experiment and participates in it directly, we might someday want to check up on how it is proceeding.

The Seas of Earth

Earth is the water world, the only celestial object we know where liquid water exists in abundance. (Later we shall discuss Jupiter's moon Europa as a possible exception to this statement.) Life on Earth began in a watery environment, and to this day the architecture of every living creature reflects this origin. All living cells are essentially bags of water in which the complex molecules essential to life can float and interact. When we dream of life on other planets, the first serious questions to ask are: Where are the oceans? Where is the water?

Why does our Earth have oceans, while the other planets do not? Since water

The Galileo spacecraft photographed Earth and its moon, performing their monthly waltz as they orbit the sun.

consists of two abundant types of atoms--hydrogen and oxygen–that appear throughout the solar system, the absence of liquid water does not occur because planets lack
the raw materials for water. Many of them do possess significant amounts of water,
but not in liquid form. Frozen and gaseous water exists on Mars, Jupiter, and Saturn,
as well as in the atmospheres of the larger moons of Saturn and Jupiter. To make
lakes of liquid water, however, requires the right temperatures (those that lie
between 32 and 212 degrees Fahrenheit), the proper atmospheric pressure, and a surface on which liquids can pool and collect.

   In other words, oceans require a planet with the right location, the right atmosphere, and a solid surface. On Venus, closer to the sun than Earth, the atmosphere's
tremendous greenhouse effect has added to the planet's natural warmth, creating a
high-temperature situation in which liquid water cannot possibly exist. On Mars, the
temperature often rises to the point where liquid water could exist, but the atmospheric pressure does not. Instead, the surface pressure remains so low that if ice
warms to 32 degrees Fahrenheit, it immediately turns to gas, much as frozen carbon
dioxide ("dry ice") passes directly from a solid to a gas at the Earth's surface. Farther
from the sun, Jupiter and Saturn have temperatures below their surfaces that include
the range where liquid water can exist, but their pressures are not the right ones, and
they lack solid surfaces on which liquid water could collect. A happy concatenation
of events—a distance from the sun that leads to liquid-water temperatures, plus an
atmosphere with sufficient pressure to keep water liquid, and a solid surface on
which liquids can collect as oceans—has produced the seas of Earth, the seas that
gave us birth and which might be essential, with different contours and trace constituents, to life throughout the universe.

   Those seas could long ago have frozen solid were it not for a remarkable property
of water: ice floats. Unlike almost all other liquids, which grow denser when they
freeze, water possesses the property of expanding its volume at temperatures low
enough to turn liquid into solid, so that water ice has only 92 percent the density of

liquid water. If ice sank, the ocean bottoms, shielded from sunlight by the overlying layers of water, would steadily accumulate ice, until the seas grew shallow, or disappeared entirely at high latitudes. But because ice floats, the ice that appears when part of the ocean freezes remains exposed to the sun's light and warmth, and often melts back into water. The modest price we must pay for this wonderful fact consists of the danger that icebergs pose to ocean-going ships, but the cinematic payoff makes even this worthwhile.

Because oceans—or at least large pools of liquid water—seem essential to life, the most fundamental question, from a search-for-life viewpoint, to ask about another planet is simply: Does it have oceans? The other objects in our solar system offer a negative reply, with only one possible exception. Does this mean that oceans themselves might be a rare phenomenon in planetary systems throughout the universe? Astronomers would dearly love to answer this question by finding oceans on planets around other stars—a dream that might be fulfilled during the first half of the new century.

Moving Plates on the Crust of Earth

Though we were born in the seas, we live on the land. Intuition tells us that our planet's uppermost surface, the Earth's crust, is the place where important things happen. In this instance, intuition is not far wrong: The interior of Earth has remained roughly the same ever since the heavier elements migrated into the core as the planet formed. Surrounding this core, which occupies the innermost one-eighth of the Earth's volume, the Earth's rocky mantle fills most of the interior, stretching from halfway out from the center almost to the surface. Atop the mantle lies the Earth's crust, 5 to 15 miles thick, not yet completely pierced by even the deepest boreholes.

Far from forming a single, solid unit, our planet's crust consists of separate plates, some as large as a continent, others as small as Texas. Driven by hot rocky material

The collision of Earth's crustal plates has lifted the Andes Mountains.

rising from the mantle below, these crustal plates glide over the mantle at speeds measured in inches per year. Some plates are colliding, raising mountain ranges such as the Himalayas by their impacts; others are sliding over one another, burying the lower plate to conceal whatever geological evidence it contains; and still other plates are gliding past one another, as is the case in California, where the Pacific and North American plates meet along the San Andreas fault line. Where one plate meets another, volcanoes tend to erupt, as they do along what geologists like to call the "ring of fire," which extends around the Pacific Ocean from New Zealand and New Guinea to the Philippines and Japan, through the Kamchatka Peninsula and the Aleutian Islands, and down the Pacific coast of America from Alaska to Tierra del Fuego.

The crust is considerably thinner beneath the seas than below the continents. As a result, the hot magma from the mantle rises beneath the oceans, not beneath the continents, to produce seafloor spreading along rifts such as the 10,000-mile-long Mid-Atlantic Ridge that runs almost from the North Pole to the South Pole. Before geologists understood the mechanism of seafloor spreading, the theory of "continental drift," first proposed by Alfred Wegener, seemed untenable, a scenario without an explanation. Today, having perceived how hot magma wells upward from the mantle, geologists have adopted Wegener's basic concept, renaming it "plate tectonics" (in Greek, *tecton* means "to change" or "to build," as in the word architect). Plate-tectonic motions have gradually moved all the older rocks on Earth away from the locations where they originally formed, posing fine problems for geologists to solve in reconstructing the tectonic history of our planet. We find ancient sea floors at high altitudes, complete with fossils of the bottom-dwelling life they once supported, discoveries that once posed a dilemma to those who knew only of Noah's flood, and that now help us to reconstruct the history of life on Earth.

If Earth had no oceans, it would still have plate-tectonic activity, similar to that discovered on Venus by the Magellan spacecraft. The existence of oceans on Earth produces the distinction between the thinner seafloor and thicker continental plates, without altering the basic process, the upwelling of hot magma from the mantle, that drives the plates' motions. The fundamental cause of plate-tectonic motions thus resides in the heating of rocks in the upper mantle. This heating in turn derives from the presence of radioactive minerals, mainly those rich in uranium and thorium, throughout the mantle. As these radioactive elements decay over time scales measured in billions of years, they release the heat that moves the pieces of the Earth's crust. Eventually—long after the sun has died—the mantle will grow poor in radioactive elements, and plate-tectonic motions will cease to jostle the plates of Earth.

When Big Things Strike the Earth

Even so, the Earth's crust will continue to undergo cosmic bombardment. As the Earth orbits the sun, it offers a target to other objects that move along intersecting orbits. Every day, tons of meteoritic dust strike our planet, and a few relatively large objects survive their passage through the atmosphere to reach its surface. Every few years, a meteoroid as large as an automobile hits the Earth; every century or so, an object the size of a house meets our planet; on a time scale measured in millennia, we can expect to encounter still larger objects, such as the one whose impact produced Arizona's Meteor Crater, nearly a mile across, some 40,000 years ago.

We may count ourselves fortunate that the amounts of debris moving in orbits that intersect the Earth decrease as we look to larger and larger objects. Because all of the objects noted above have relatively small sizes, none of them can be detected before striking the Earth with our present technological capabilities. If we seek to improve our ability to discover and to track potential impacting objects, we probably ought to devote our greatest efforts into discovering and following the objects that can inflict the most damage to our planet.

Those are, of course, objects much larger than the one that dug Meteor Crater, so large that they are called asteroids or comets rather than meteoroids. Even the impact that made Meteor Crater, devastating though it might have been locally, almost certainly had no global effect. We should fear not objects tens of yards in diameter, which can excavate such a crater, but rather the mile-wide objects, whose impacts will affect our entire planet. The primary effects of these impacts arise not from their shaking the Earth (though their impacts would be felt around the world) but rather from the changes in the Earth's climate that their debris causes for months or even years afterward.

Collisions between the Earth and a mile-wide object occur every million years or so, whereas an object five to ten miles across strikes the Earth every 30 to 50 million years, on the average. The best-known impact in the latter category made the Chicxulub crater in the Yucatán peninsula of Mexico, nearly a hundred miles across, and partly buried beneath the Gulf of Mexico. Sixty-five million years ago, a comet or asteroid about six miles across smashed into the Earth at a speed of many thousand miles per hour to raise some worldwide, unholy hell. As the object bored toward the Earth, it created a hole in the atmosphere; much of the debris ejected from the Earth's surface by the impact spewed upward through this hole, coated the top of the atmosphere like an oil slick, and then slowly settled back to Earth.

The larger grains of dust sank to the surface within weeks, but the smallest ones must have taken months to do so, keeping sunlight dim over much of the Earth's surface, where great storms may have been raging in response to the sudden change in the environment. Because this cosmic catastrophe coincided in time with the "mass extinction" that occurred at the end of the Cretaceous era—an extinction that embraced every type of dinosaur, as well as many other living species—we may reasonably identify this impact as the cause of the mass extinction. This identification in turn suggests that most, if not all, of the earlier mass extinctions, such as the one more than 200 million years ago that ended the Permian era and killed off an even higher percentage of all living species than the dinosaur extinction did, may have occurred because of collisions with objects more than a few miles across. However, no impact craters have been securely identified as coincident in time with those earlier extinctions, though this may be simply because the effects of plate tectonics and erosion have removed all traces of the crater.

When will the next life-destroying impact occur? Statistically speaking, only after a few million, or tens of millions, of years. If we seek to be more specific, we must discover and track all the objects at least a mile or so in diameter that may eventually strike the Earth. Astronomers have projects now underway to do so, but they consider themselves underfunded in their efforts. False alarms such as the one in March 1998, when a mile-wide object called 1997 XF11 was first heralded as a possible impactor and then dismissed as certain to miss the Earth, might be seen as attempts to draw publicity to the desirability of finding all the relatively large objects that might encounter our planet, and then determining when and if they might actually do so. The probity of astronomers, as well as the opprobrium that attached when astronomers seemed unable to calculate an orbit correctly, speaks against the notion that a plot might have been underway to raise public awareness of the fact that a comet or asteroid may prove to be on a collision course with Earth. We may anticipate significant improvement, during the next few decades, in our catalogs of possible Earth impactors.

And what if we do find that a large object will slam into our planet? First, we shall need a committee, which we may fervently hope will adopt a coherent, planetwide strategy. With any luck, astronomers' abilities to calculate the future course of an asteroid from observations made during past years will provide many years, or even many decades, to prepare a plan. This plan might include sending nuclear explosives to the impactor, then detonating them in a way that nudges the object into a new orbit, one that is free of any direct meeting with Earth. But who can assure us that mistakes will not be made, so that what is meant to deflect an impact actually ends up causing one? Can we be sure that the detonation will not leave large fragments of the object still on a collision course? These questions will demand serious answers, and we may hope that no splinter governments decide, for example, that although others judge an asteroid not to be a threat, they must send their own explosives to it. For now, ignorance brings bliss: We know of no large objects that will strike the Earth, and our inaction has proven correct—so far.

On Earth, the traces of even the largest impacts have disappeared with the passage of billions of years, as weathering, erosion, and plate-tectonic activity have worn them away or buried them beneath plates of the crust. Those who seek a pristine record of impacts need look no farther than our satellite, which carries scars from almost every sizable object that hit it during the past 3 billion years. For example, a pair of binoculars easily reveals the 50-mile-wide lunar crater called Tycho, made when an object several miles across struck the moon nearly 100 million years ago.

Our Cratered Moon

Earth has a single moon, one-quarter the size of our planet, our companion as we orbit the sun. By far the brightest object in our night skies, the moon has delighted a thousand generations of Homo sapiens, who one generation ago sent spacecraft and human explorers to that nearby world, just 240,000 miles from Earth. As we know from watching the "man in the moon," our satellite always keeps the same side facing toward Earth. This must occur because the moon's interior has some regions denser than others, and the Earth's gravity has locked onto those denser regions, holding them toward the Earth as the moon rotates. As a result, the moon rotates in exactly the same amount of time as it takes to orbit the Earth, 27 1/3 days.

Even without a telescope, we can easily observe the two basic types of surface features on the moon. The light-colored lunar highlands are rich in craters, made by impacts during the great era of bombardment, which lasted from about 4.5 billion to 3.9 billion years ago, soon after the Earth and moon had formed.

The lunar maria are dark, wide plains of frozen lava; older, more heavily cratered terrain forms the lunar highlands.

After the final giant impacts had helped to excavate wide plains or basins, volcanic outflows produced titanic flows of lava that filled these basins to form the maria (from the Latin word for "seas," pronounced MARR-ee-ah). Similar lava flows have covered thousands of square miles in India and eastern Washington State, but the lunar maria are even larger, up to about 600 miles in diameter. Because these lava flows occurred during the few hundred million years after the great era of bombardment had ended, the lunar maria show far fewer craters than the highlands, though they carry the full record of the last 3 billion years of impacts on the moon.

The moon has essentially no atmosphere, so nothing buffers the temperature changes that arise as the two-week-long lunar day becomes an equally long lunar night. During this cycle, the moon's surface temperature rises and falls by hundreds of degrees, from a daytime temperature of 250 degrees Fahrenheit to a nighttime temperature close to 180 degrees below zero. Visitors to the moon must carry thermal shielding as well as all the food, air, and water they consume, making lunar exploration an expensive undertaking.

Exploring the Moon

The dawn of the space age brought our first look at the far side of the moon, which no human saw until 1959, when the Soviet spacecraft Luna 3 passed behind the moon and sent photographs of its hidden face to Earth by radio. The lunar far-side turned out to consist primarily of highland terrain, with almost none of the maria that cover about one-third of the moon's near side. Astronomers still hope to explain this asymmetry, perhaps in terms of the density differences that keep the moon's rotational and orbital periods locked together.

The first terrestrial spacecraft to reach the moon (the Soviet Luna 9) landed in 1966; three years later, men reached the moon for the first time, as part of the U.S. Apollo program. The NASA astronauts' sixth and final trip to the moon occurred in 1972; since then, our satellite has remained free of human contact.

On their six journeys, the astronauts collected several hundred pounds of lunar rock samples for careful study in Earth-bound laboratories, a task that could have been accomplished far more cheaply and efficiently with robotic spacecraft. Human nature, however, focuses on exploits that prominently feature human beings, though the public has begun to notice that an automated spacecraft on Mars has far more to tell us than an astronaut circling a few hundred miles above the Earth. We may someday find the money and energy to send human beings—along with the vast quantities of water, food, and oxygen they require—to neighboring planets, but for now we must rely on our ever better automated instruments, which have brought us discovery after discovery from worlds billions of miles away.

Did the Moon Form from a Giant Impact on Earth?

Striking though they may be, the impacts of six- or nine-mile-wide objects with Earth pale into insignificance when compared to the mother of all impacts (so far as planetary theorizing goes), the cosmic collision hypothesized to explain the formation of the moon. To this day, how the moon formed remains a mystery to astronomers, who have now managed to characterize their theories into three basic possibilities. The moon may have formed as a "sister" of Earth, an object that gradually aggregated in the vicinity of our planet; or as a "daughter" of Earth, assembled from a chunk blasted loose from our planet; or as a "stranger" to Earth, made somewhere else in the solar system and captured by Earth's gravity long afterward. Though one of these scenarios seems almost certain to prove correct, all three must be rated as "improbable," as Harold Urey, Nobel-prizewinning planetary scientist, once pronounced.

Though Urey has passed on, living astronomers have careers to maintain. They have come to favor the daughter hypothesis for the moon's origin, with a wrinkle. According to the current scenario, the late stages in agglomerating the planets, about 4.5 billion years ago, was a time when enormous chunks of debris still orbited the sun in large numbers. These objects made the Earth's neighborhood a dangerous place, for their orbits were changing rapidly (on astronomical time scales) as the multitude of newly formed objects interacted with one another gravitationally. Suppose that one of these objects, with a mass comparable to that of Mars (one-tenth of the

Earth's mass) collided with our planet. Such an enormous collision would have ejected large amounts of matter into orbit relatively close to the Earth; much of this material could then have coalesced to form our moon. The collision would have thrown the impacting object into a new orbit, perhaps to be consumed by a newborn giant planet, perhaps to be flung entirely out of the solar system.

Could have, would have—what does this scenario offer us beyond the fecund imagination of planetary scientists? The scenario rests on well-established evidence, painstakingly gathered and analyzed from the lunar surface, and from computer simulations of planetary impacts and their results. The only difficulty with this pat answer is that the evidence points in several directions, but it does seem to favor a daughter origin of the moon. The most significant evidence consists of the composition of the lunar rocks brought to Earth during the early 1970s. These samples contain minerals similar to those on Earth, which suggest a common origin for the lunar and terrestrial rocks. Going beyond suggestion, the elements in these rocks appear in several isotopes, different versions of the same element. Oxygen, for example, exists in three different isotopes—oxygen-16, oxygen-17, and oxygen-18—all of which consist of atoms whose nuclei each contain 8 protons, but also include either 8, 9, or 10 neutrons. The neutrons mark the different isotopes, and the ratio of the abundances in which the isotopes occur gives each chunk of matter a cosmic fingerprint, which we may hope to use to identify where the rocks were made.

In their ratios of different isotopes, the rocks from the moon show a remarkable resemblance to Earth rocks, and differ significantly from the isotope ratios measured on Mars by the Viking spacecraft. This resemblance argues for a common origin for the rocks, but another fact speaks against it. Compared to the Earth's surface, the lunar material contains far less volatile material, which vaporizes easily when heated. In classifying solids, physicists and chemists specify their overall properties with the ratio of volatile to nonvolatile matter. Water is the best-known volatile; other volatile compounds include carbon monoxide, carbon dioxide, and other simple molecules formed when carbon combines with other elements. Thus the moon rocks present us with a conundrum: The details of their composition (the isotope abundance ratios) closely resemble those on Earth, but the bulk properties of their matter (the ratio of volatile to nonvolatile material) deviate substantially from what we find on Earth.

The answer lies, astronomers tell us, in the invocation of the right sort of giant collision to form the moon. This collision must have blasted enormous amounts of matter loose from our planet, leaving much of it in orbit, and—here is the wrinkle in the daughter theory—the material that entered Earth orbit must have been volatile-poor. The latter proviso seems reasonable, since the ejected material must have been heated to high temperatures by the force of the impact. At temperatures of a few hundred degrees, the volatile material would have become gaseous and had an excellent chance of escaping into interplanetary space. The nonvolatile material, left in orbit around the Earth, could then coalesce to form our moon.

Calculations imply that this sort of impact and coalescence might indeed have produced the moon we find today. However, these calculations imply that the moon's orbit around the Earth has grown significantly larger. In the favored scenario, the moon should have formed at less than one-tenth of its present distance from Earth, because only there would the density of matter been sufficiently large to allow the moon to coalesce from debris within an astronomically likely period of time. We do know that the moon is slowly receding from Earth as the result of tidal interactions between the Earth and moon, so we can easily assign the ancient moon a closer position; but a location so close to Earth bends some astronomers' minds a bit too far. For now, however, the favored scenario is the one described above, making the Earth and moon extremely close neighbors as the moon began to form.

Is There Water on the Moon?

Early in 1998, the Lunar Prospector spacecraft briefly electrified the world—or at least that portion dreaming of lunar colonies—by finding evidence of ice near the moon's poles. This spacecraft, in orbit 60 miles above the lunar surface, carries several instruments with which to examine the lunar surface. The discovery of water was made with an instrument called a neutron spectrometer, which detects neutrons released when extremely fast-moving particles bombard matter. We can analogize this process to firing bullets at material of unknown composition and studying the fragments released by these impacts. Both the speed at which the fragments emerge and the matter they contain must depend on the material under bombardment. So it

is on the moon. There the "bullets" arrive freely and continuously, in the form of electrons, protons, and other particles moving at enormous speeds. These streams of particles, which fill the universe, carry the old-fashioned name of cosmic rays, given to them even before scientists knew that they consist of relatively familiar types of particles, but moving so rapidly that they behave in ways different from what we observe in laboratories.

The moon's north polar region contains water ice mixed into the lunar soil.

Using its neutron spectrometer, Lunar Prospector found that the craters close to the north and south poles of the moon contain ice. This does not mean that vast ice sheets cover the floors of these craters, or that chunks of ice lie like beached icebergs on the lunar surface. The proportion of ice in the soil near the moon's poles varies from 0.3 to 1 percent, according to the lunar scientists' best analysis of their data. In other words, these regions, like the rest of the moon, are made of rock, but in this case, of rock with a small admixture of ice.

At least two ways exist to describe the new discovery. On the one hand, the lunar surface apparently includes tens of millions of tons of water, frozen for billions of years in the form of ice, at each of its two polar regions. If we plan to send humans to live on the moon, this ice could prove a most valuable resource. Extracted from the rock and then either melted into water or separated into its hydrogen and oxygen components, the ice could provide not only drinking water but also oxygen to breathe. Every ton of ice could furnish a colonist with roughly half a year's supply of air and water, or a couple of months' worth if the colonist plans to bathe regularly. Thus a thousand colonists could last for a thousand years before exhausting the lunar ice, and even a million colonists could survive for a year at the moon's poles before the ice ran out. These time periods must be reduced, perhaps by a factor of three to ten, if we also plan to use the water extracted from the moon's surface for agriculture in lunar hothouses, theoretically capable of producing food for the colonists.

On the other hand, we may have some qualms about digging up the moon's poles to extract the ice in the soil, and still greater reservations about whether this extraction would be cost-effective. Since the ice lies dispersed over roughly 10,000 square miles of lunar surface at each pole, we must envision machines to till these expanses of lunar soil, separating ice from a quantity of rock at least a hundred times greater. Then the ice must be processed into water and oxygen in order to obtain the essential ingredients for human colonization. Currently, and well into the foreseeable future, it will be cheaper to send water and oxygen from Earth than to attack the moon for these necessaries. In view of the limited supply of lunar ice (at least when colonists number in the many hundreds or thousands), we might do well to set aside the moon's poles as an inner-solar-system ice reserve. Even this could be seen as greedy by other civilizations who might have an eye on the lunar ice, but fortunately (from this angle at least), we know of no such other civilizations.

The Sun, the Moon, and the Tides

With the exception of Pluto's moon, Charon, Earth's satellite ranks as the largest of all moons, judged in comparison to their planets. None of Jupiter's moons, for example, have masses even as large as 1/1,000 of Jupiter's, while our satellite, with 1/81 of the Earth's mass, ranks more than a dozen times higher on the moon-planet mass ratio. The moon's relatively large mass allows it to produce important effects on our planet. For our daily routines, by far the most significant effect consists of the tides that the moon raises on Earth.

Tides result from the gravitational forces that one object exerts on another. However—and here we face a subtlety that can baffle the unwary—the tides arise not from gravity pure and simple but rather from differences in the amount of gravitational forces. These in turn arise from differences in the distances from one object to another. To choose the obvious example, as the moon orbits the Earth, its gravity pulls on all of our planet, but it pulls most strongly on the parts of Earth closest to the moon, with somewhat less force on the Earth's center, and with the least amount of force on the parts of the Earth that lie on the opposite side of the center. Because of these different amounts of force, the Earth tends to bulge like a football, extending itself toward the moon and also away from it. Those who encounter this explanation tend to agree that the Earth ought to bulge toward the moon—but why should it have a symmetric bulge away from it? Some reflection, though, may show that the situation is indeed symmetric, and as the differences in force pull the "near" side of Earth away from its center, they also pull the center away from the "far" side.

Hence the Earth always exhibits a tidal bulge, a distortion along the line joining the centers of the Earth and moon, that swells the Earth both toward the moon and away from it. Because the oceans can respond more readily than the land does to the differences in force, we observe this tidal bulge as the sloshing of the oceans with respect to the shore. As the Earth rotates, a seaside observer will see two high tides and two low tides every day, because he will encounter both the bulge toward the moon and the bulge away. More precisely, the cycle of tides takes about 24 hours and 50 minutes—the same length of time required for the moon to regain its original position in the sky. The difference between this period and 24 hours arises because the moon keeps moving in its orbit around the Earth.

If the seashores of Earth had no bends, any observer would see high tide occur at whenever the moon rose to its highest point in the sky, and also halfway between these times, when the observer's location faced directly away from the moon. Because the shoreline bends and twists, the tides must take some time in running up and down the coast, always lagging somewhat behind the tides that would occur in an idealized world. Particular topography can funnel the tidal waters, producing spectacular differences between times of high and low tides, as occurs in the Bay of Fundy, where 30-foot differences in sea level routinely appear.

True lovers of the tides know that some weeks bring larger-than-average tide changes, while others see reduced effects. Here we see the interplay of the moon with the sun, which also raises tides on Earth. Even though the sun exerts far more gravitational force than the moon does (hence we orbit the sun), when we calculate the differences in the amounts of force arising from these two objects, the moon wins by more than a factor of two. At times close to full moon and new moon, the sun and moon combine their effects, producing especially large "spring tides" that rise higher and fall lower than the usual ones. Close to the first-quarter and last-quarter phases of the moon, the sun's tidal effects partially cancel the moon's, resulting in "neap tides," when the tides seem to take a nap, as the etymology suggests.

Life on Earth may well have begun in tide pools, first awash in seawater and then drained of it. This alternation might have been the key to the assemblage of complex molecules, eventually capable of self-replication. Although this tide-pool hypothesis for the origin of life remains speculative, even the possibility of proving correct emphasizes how a modest effect, dependent on a celestial coincidence such as the possession of a large moon, could prove crucial in determining whether a planet teems with vitality or reeks with lifelessness.

MARS

One planet has fascinated humanity throughout recorded history, and has remained the chief focus for speculation about life beyond Earth: rust red Mars. Mars intrigued our ancestors long before they had any correct notion of what Mars is or is like; Mars captivated the public a century ago, when astronomers' reports of civilization-made canals burst into the public arena; and Mars has remained the center of attention in our efforts to find extraterrestrial life in the solar system. Though Europa and Titan have a chance to claim the top spot in this search, Mars has lost none of its allure. Burnished by fiction and buttressed by fact, the hunt for life on Mars continues, with arguably greater prospects in the space age than ever before.

Fourth Rock from the Sun

Just over half the size of Earth, with one-tenth Earth's mass and a surface gravitational force only 40 percent of the Earth's, Mars is the second smallest of the basic eight planets that orbit the sun. Even a size chauvinist may note, however, that because Mars has no oceans, its land surface nearly equals that on Earth, and offers prime real estate for those who have no development qualms and an unlimited budget. Mars nearly matches Earth in its rotation period (just over 24 $1/2$ hours) and in the angle at which its rotation axis tilts as it orbits the sun (by 25 degrees from the perpendicular to the plane of its orbit, while Earth tilts by 23 $1/2$ degrees). Mars therefore has a day-and-night cycle and seasonal variations that closely resemble those on Earth. But these Earth-Mars resemblances in land area and rotation cannot overcome the planetary differences that arise from Mars's diminutive size. Because the thin Martian atmosphere cannot keep water liquid, Mars's surface has become a dusty, apparently lifeless plain, humped with hills and rocks, but without a single watery rill, rivulet, or river.

Mars apparently owes its small size to the fact that it orbits the sun at just over 1.5 times the Earth-sun distance, taking nearly two years for each orbit. This puts Mars uncomfortably close to the giant among the sun's planets, Jupiter, whose mass equals 3,000 times the mass of Mars. Jupiter orbits the sun at 5.2 times the Earth's distance, compared with Mars's 1.52 times. Even so, just as Jupiter's gravitational force denied the asteroids (orbiting, on average, at 2.8 times the Earth's distance from the sun) the chance to collect themselves into a planet, it also prevented much of the material that could otherwise have joined proto-Mars from doing so.

Small though it may be, Mars is no pygmy. Its surface possesses remarkable features, none so remarkable, of course, as the imagined canals that once mesmerized those who dream of civilizations beyond the Earth. The notion of Martian canals originated with the Italian astronomer Giovanni Schiaparelli, who reported that he had seen *canali*, a word best translated as "straight lines," on the red planet. Even a limited imagination could build fantastic structures upon this report, and no one did so with greater effect than Percival Lowell (one of the Boston Lowells), who had already gained fame and fortune from well-written books about his long residence and travels in Korea and Japan. Fascinated by Schiaparelli's report, and by the possibility of life on Mars, Lowell searched for the best observing location in America to erect his privately funded telescope. On Mars Hill, the site he chose near Flagstaff, Arizona, Lowell devoted many years, just over a century ago, to making fine drawings of our planetary neighbor. Lowell's maps showed a dense network of canals, some of them double, often meeting at junctions of three or more canals. Lowell insisted that these canals must be the engineering feats of an advanced, water-hungry civilization, giant trenches built to carry water from the Martian polar caps to dry regions near the equator.

Lowell's work strongly influenced the English writer H. G. Wells, whose classic book *War of the Worlds* describes the invasion of Earth by Martians eager for plunder and water, a theme developed by countless science-fiction movies, including a seminal film from the 1950s that brought Wells's book to life. A still more famous Martian invasion (at least among those who study urban folklore) occurred on October 30, 1938, when Orson Welles and the Mercury Radio Theater of the Air broadcast a dramatization of Wells's novel, moving the key Martian attack point to New Jersey and causing panic among thousands of listeners along the East Coast, many of whom fled for their lives without checking other radio stations for advice. Before long (and no doubt after confronting the fact that Earth has no good direction in which to run from an alien intrusion), the realization spread that humanity remained safe, at least for a time, from all but its own invasions.

Lowell's Martian canals touched a deep vein of human longing for, and fear of, contact with extraterrestrial civilizations. For seven decades, from the end of the nineteenth century to the mid-1960s, debate continued over the existence of Martian canals, or at least long, straight topographic features. Some observers saw these lines

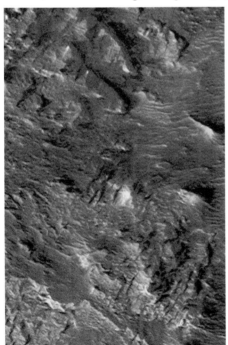

while others did not. Spacecraft observations, beginning with Mariner 4 in 1965, finally laid the canals to rest, revealing a surface unexpectedly dotted with a host of craters, but without a canal in sight. The canals drawn by Lowell and many other Mars observers apparently arose from the human brain's tendency (verified by many experiments) to create order from visual chaos—in this case, to combine indistinct features into straight lines. With the canals' demise also died any claim that Mars has an advanced civilization now, though the power of human imagination then shifted to long-vanished ones, exemplified by the "Face on Mars."

NASA's Mars Global Surveyor spacecraft is now mapping the red planet with high-resolution photography

The Real Mars: A Fine Landscape Without Water

The real Mars, revealed to human eyes by spacecraft exploration, turns out to be a planet of awesome desolation, with enormous, extinct volcanoes, an immense canyon nearly as wide as the United States, and a cratered surface enveloped in a thin atmosphere made mainly of carbon dioxide. Let us make a quick reconnaissance of the Martian surface, meeting the chief facts about conditions on the red planet.

First of all, Mars is cold! At its warmest equatorial locations, in the full Martian summer, the surface warms nearly to room temperature at noon, suggesting an environment pleasant to Earth life. Even there, however, the onset of night brings a 150-degree temperature drop that makes the surface far colder than the Arctic in winter. The chilling occurs because Mars's atmosphere, even though it consists primarily of carbon-dioxide molecules that trap infrared radiation efficiently, is so thin that the effects of daylight heating radiate away within a few hours.

Second, Mars is indeed red. Most of the surface has the characteristic rust red color that arises from the combination of iron compounds in its soil with oxygen in its atmosphere. In other words, the Martian surface is slowly rusting away, like the similarly colored rocks in the Grand Canyon. Not every Martian rock has a reddish hue, but most of them contain sufficient iron to show the effects of slow oxidation—proof that Mars does have some oxygen in its thin, mostly carbon-dioxide atmosphere.

Mars has ancient volcanoes, the largest mountains in the solar system, which have all been extinct for billions of years, and whose presence demonstrates that the planet once had plate-tectonic activity and reservoirs of hot magma. Mars also has polar caps, much thinner than Earth's, which consist primarily of frozen carbon dioxide, much colder than water ice. Some summers see one of the Martian polar caps evaporate completely—proof that it can be only a few yards thick. Mixed in with the frozen carbon dioxide, Mars does have a small amount of water ice in its polar caps—

not enough with which to plan a large Martian colony, but nevertheless present in significant amounts.

What Mars does not have anywhere on its surface is liquid water. Why not? Liquid water cannot exist on the Martian surface because the atmospheric pressure equals only 6 or 7 millibars—0.6 or 0.7 percent of the pressure at Earth's surface. This amount falls below the minimum pressure that allows water to exist as a liquid at any temperature. Instead, ice whose temperature rises above 32 degrees Fahrenheit promptly vaporizes, and any water vapor that cools below the freezing point will freeze directly into solid ice, skipping any transition through the liquid state.

The Vikings Explore the Red Planet

We now know that Mars did have liquid water on its surface billions of years ago. The proof of this fact reached Earth more than two decades ago, when two Viking orbiters photographed the planet's entire surface and sent two landers to dig into the Martian soil and test it for life.

Photographs from the Viking orbiters revealed winding channels, which geologists believe must have been made by flows of liquid; they also showed dried-up lake beds and regions in which a sudden rush of liquid has left behind a broad flood plain. The only liquid reasonably likely to have existed on Mars is water, made from two of the most abundant

The Viking orbiters photographed regions where running water has shaped the landscape.

elements in the solar system. Mars almost certainly never had planet-wide oceans, but 4 billion years ago, the planet had active volcanoes, which should have belched forth some of the gases that had been trapped in Mars's subsurface layers. This volcanic outpouring should have made the atmosphere sufficiently thick for liquid water to have existed on Mars.

The gases most likely to have formed a thick Martian atmosphere are carbon dioxide and water vapor, which still provide the bulk of today's thin atmosphere. If Mars's atmosphere contained these two gases in amounts sufficient to double the current atmospheric pressure, then liquid water could exist at temperatures between 32 to 38 degrees Fahrenheit. If the Martian atmosphere contained 10 times the amount of carbon dioxide that it does now, its atmospheric pressure would rise tenfold, to 6 percent of Earth's surface pressure; this would broaden the temperature range for liquid water, so that it would run from 32 to about 70 degrees Fahrenheit. Primitive Mars probably had pressures like these, with abundant liquid water on its surface and water vapor in its atmosphere. The greater amounts of carbon dioxide and water vapor in its atmosphere would also have increased the greenhouse effect, giving Mars a warmer surface.

What happened to this demi-paradise of primitive Mars? Where did the water go? Some of Mars's carbon dioxide may have escaped into space, while more of it froze into the Martian polar caps. Some of the water vapor also escaped, while a tiny amount of it joined the dry ice of the polar caps. Much of the water probably remains widely distributed over the planet in the form of ice, not on but *under* the Martian surface. This surface may resemble the permafrost of Alaska and Siberia, which contain large amounts of ice intermingled with the soil beneath the surface.

1976: The Viking Search for Life on Mars

When scientists confronted their long-awaited opportunity to search for life on Mars, they had to develop experiments to detect unknown forms of life. To do so, the Viking biologists drew on their knowledge of the regions where our planet most closely resembles Mars, the dry valleys of Antarctica, the coldest and driest locations on Earth. There, biologists have discovered tiny organisms called cryptoendoliths ("hidden inside the rocks"). Cryptoendoliths are colonies of interacting lichens that take shelter just below the surfaces of rocks from the harsh temperature and rapid temperature changes that rule the outside world. The Viking scientists had to design instruments to test for organisms as exotic and hard-stressed as the cryptoendoliths, but with a range of detection that could find even stranger living creatures. What instruments could they pack into their miniature, automated laboratories for a trip to Mars?

Perhaps the most basic and essential instruments brought to Mars by the Viking landers to search for life were their camera systems, which obtained thousands of images of the planet's surface at the two landing sites. None of them showed a single trace of life, not a creature, corpse, trail, burrow, skeleton, or waste product. This might simply show, however, that life on Mars, like most of life on Earth, is microscopic in size. For this reason, each Viking lander carried a miniaturized laboratory —unfortunately not equipped with a microscope, which had been rated as too expensive, too difficult to operate, and with too little potential benefit. Instead, scientists relied not on visual but on *chemical* evidence for the existence of life.

What chemical evidence would be most decisive? Deciding what constitutes proof of life cannot be resolved to everyone's satisfaction. The farther we get from familiar forms of life, the more difficult becomes the definition of life. The Viking scientists, entirely familiar with this problem, had to wrestle with the fundamental question, What is life? No simple answer exists, but a reasonable stab might be: Life consists of systems capable of both reproduction and evolution. But who had the time to look for either of these? Could other signs of life prove definitive?

The Viking scientists decided to look for the results of any life forms' breathing or eating, or for corpses. Their breathing experiment dripped a set of chemical compounds labeled by radioactivity onto the soil, then looked for telltale signs that microbes in the soil had "breathed out" some of the labeled compounds. The eating experiment dropped Martian soil into a broth of several dozen likely nutrients, then searched for changes in the gas immediately above the broth, to show that microbes had incorporated at least some of the liquid. The search for corpses first exposed Martian soil to an atmosphere in which radioactive carbon replaced ordinary carbon, then roasted the soil to see whether it had gained any radioactive carbon as organisms ingested carbon compounds from the air. With these three experiments, Viking had a good chance to find any organisms that breathed or ate or produced corpses with organic (carbon-containing) material.

Impressively, all three life-detecting experiments at both locations showed positive results! Yet few of the scientists concluded that microbes exist on Mars. Instead, they recognized, with the sudden clarity of hindsight, the immense difficulties involved in distinguishing chemical changes caused by life from those caused by nonliving processes—especially when this distinction aims at finding an unknown form of life. The consensus emerged that the chemistry of the Martian soil has mimicked what living creatures on Mars might do.

The Viking experiments did include another, possible crucial instrument, designed to measure the amounts of different types of molecules in the Martian soil and atmosphere. This instrument, called a mass spectrometer, showed that Martian soil contains no carbon-based molecules, similar to the organic molecules found in living organisms on Earth, down to a level of a few parts per billion, the best accuracy that the spectrometer could attain. Even Antarctic soil, far from any living creatures, contains a small amount of this organic material, which either arises from the decay of long-vanished creatures or floats down from the atmosphere. The lack of any organic compounds weighs in the balance against the existence of life on Mars, even though, by itself, it does not disprove it.

What do the results of the Viking landings on Mars now tell us? Almost all the biologists who have looked carefully at the Viking results conclude that chemistry on Mars duplicated the biological activity that the miniature laboratories had been designed to detect, and that the Martian soil sampled by the landers contains no life at all. These experts might, of course, be wrong. One well-known member of the Viking team, the biologist Gilbert Levin, has concluded that Martian microbes do offer the most likely explanation for the results from the Vikings' life-detection experiments. But all of Levin's cohorts maintain the opposite: that the positive results from each of the three experiments find their best explanation in chemical reactions that mimic the activity of microorganisms on Earth.

Could Life Still Exist on Mars?

With the exception of Levin and a few others, scientists found the Viking results dashed hopes of finding that life now exists on Mars. They all agreed, however, that billions of years ago, primitive Mars was far more favorable to life, so much so that the results of present-day searches took nothing away from the possibility of ancient life on Mars. The difference lies in the presence or absence of liquid water.

Without liquid water, we cannot expect life. Let us promptly modify this thought with two little exceptions. First, another substance, such as ammonia or methyl alcohol, could allow molecules to float and to interact within it, playing the role of a "solvent," as water does for life on Earth. However, water does seem to provide the finest solvent, both in terms of a solvent's function and also as the solvent most easily made from abundant atoms throughout the cosmos. Second, some forms of life require liquid water only during the crucial stages, not at all times. The conclusion seems strong that we can expect to find life only where we can find at least *some* liquid water.

Does this mean that no life can exist on Mars? Not at all! We can imagine life that has found a niche beneath the polar caps or in subterranean caverns heated by the last remnants of Mars's volcanic activity. These underground oases, though entirely imaginary, rank high on the list of places to search for when spacecraft return to Mars. Furthermore, life might exist throughout all of the Martian subsurface, where large amounts of water have probably become permanently frozen in the soil. This permafrost would resemble the Siberian tundra, where colonies of bacteria can thrive hundreds of yards beneath the surface, because the local conditions allow tiny amounts of water to be liquid at any moment.

We may seem to be stretching things in favor of finding life by imagining Martian life in a permafrost even harsher than Siberia's. Yet the investigation of life on Earth has continually revealed unexpected forms of life, capable of adapting to, and surviving in, conditions that once seemed impossible. Biologists have therefore learned to be cautious in pronouncing a situation totally unfit for life. Their approach seemed vindicated one fine summer day when the news spread around the Earth that NASA scientists claimed to have found evidence for life on Mars in a rock from Antarctica.

ALH 84001: One Fine Rock from Mars

How could anyone know that a particular rock came from Mars? And how could anyone conclude that this rock contains evidence of life existing on another planet, billions of years ago?

ALH 84001 could be identified as a meteorite from Mars by measuring the amounts of various atomic isotopes contained in the rock. The ratios of these isotopes differ slightly but significantly from those of Earth rocks, but they correspond to the abundance ratios that the Viking spacecraft measured on Mars. Since Mars never approaches the Earth within 30 million miles, ALH 84001, like the eleven other meteorites identified as Martian in origin, must have been blasted from the Martian surface by an impact. After millions of years in orbit around the sun (geologists can estimate this time by the effects produced in the rock from its exposure to the fast-moving particles that permeate interplanetary space), ALH 84001 happened to strike the Earth, where it lay on the Antarctic ice for more than ten thousand years before a meteorite hunter named Roberta Score found it during the Antarctic summer of 1984–85 and gave it a year and number label. Once the rock was recognized as Martian, more than a decade later, meteoriticists gave it special attention. Their radioactive age-dating techniques put this Martian rock into a category by itself: ALH 84001 is 4.3 billion years old, more than three times older than any other meteorite from Mars.

Far more intriguing than its age is the fact that ALH 84001 includes microscopic orange-colored spheres whose rims show alternating layers of light and dark material. Careful analysis of these rims showed that (1) the material contains molecules of PAHs (polycyclic aromatic hydrocarbons), which often arise on Earth as organic mat-

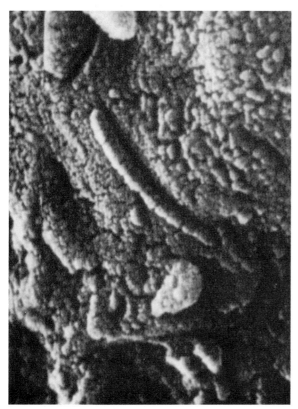

ter decays, though PAHs can also can appear in the absence of life; (2) the spheres contain tiny mineral inclusions that resemble tiny bar magnets, similar to those that are made by a class of bacteria on Earth that uses these magnetic minerals to orient themselves in our planet's magnetic field; and (3) the material at the rims of the spheres contain what David McKay, the leader of the meteorite science team at the Johnson Space Center, called "ovoids," tiny, elongated structures whose length equals only one-millionth of the width of a human hair.

What do these three facts tell us about the 4.3-billion-year-old rock

The ancient Martian meteorite ALH 84001 contains carbonate globules with tiny "ovoids" less than one millionth of an inch long.

from Mars? The evidence suggests tantalizing, but far from definitive possibilities. Ancient life on Mars might have left behind the PAH molecules, but the PAHs might also have arisen without the presence of life—or from Earthly contamination while the meteorite lay on the Antarctic ice. The magnetized minerals closely resemble what some bacterial manufacture on Earth, but we also find similar minerals made by natural processes. And the ovoids, most controversial of all, may have the shapes of living cells, but they may not even be hollow (even the finest electron microscopes cannot resolve this issue), and certainly may not be fossil cells. The ovoids' minuscule size, much smaller than those of most terrestrial cells, does not pose an absolute obstacle against their having been living cells. Basaltic rock deep below the Columbia River basin seems to contain organisms almost as small as ALH 84001's ovoids.

In 1997, the NASA committee in charge of the rock sent samples that total a few percent of the original mass of ALH 84001 to 40 groups of researchers, who each received, on average, about a pennyweight of material. These research teams continue to study this most intriguing meteorite from Mars, hoping to find more definitive evidence for and against the hypothesis that life flourished on Mars billions of years ago. Though we may hope that this evidence will emerge, or that meteorite hunters may yet find a still more fascinating rock from Mars, the debates about Martian life will most likely be settled by long, hard journeys to and from the red planet.

New Spacecraft Missions to Mars

On July 4, 1997, Mars Pathfinder—the first spacecraft to reach Mars in 21 years, and the first ever to land on Mars without first orbiting around the planet—bounced on its airbags 15 or 20 times before it came to a stop, let the airbags deflate, and exposed to the Martian environment its instruments and its little rover, named Sojourner after the famous anti-slavery and women's-rights crusader Sojourner Truth. Launched in December 1996, Mars Pathfinder was aimed at the Ares Vallis region, a

two-mile-deep valley about 60 miles long, which offered a relatively flat landing surface and also set the lander sufficiently close enough to the Martian equator for sunlight to run its solar-power cells. Sojourner ventured down the ramp and out into the
landscape, examining rocks within a few dozen yards of the Pathfinder spacecraft.
Pathfinder itself, which NASA renamed the Carl Sagan Memorial Station, recorded
the Martian weather, measured the air pressure, and studied the dust in the Martian
atmosphere. This dust turned out to be highly magnetized, hard to explain in view of
the fact that Mars now lacks a measurable magnetic field. The measured surface
temperatures ranged from minus 170 to minus 15 Fahrenheit, often varying by 35
degrees in just a few minutes.

From Pathfinder and Sojourner, which operated for more than three months on
the Martian surface, we now have a new set of images of Mars, from a region known
to be the site of ancient water flows. These pho-
tographs show a set of rocks of various sizes,
which to the untutored eye seem highly reminiscent of the scenes at the two Viking landing sites,
thousands of miles away. To experts, however, the
distribution of rock sizes at the Pathfinder site con-
firms the conclusion that Ares Vallis is a floodplain,

In 1977, the Sojourner rover investigated rocks up to a few dozen yards from the Pathfinder spacecraft.

analogous to the "Channeled Scablands" of eastern Washington State, where a mam-
moth flood once rolled rocks of all sizes along the surface. Sojourner could roll up to

individual rocks, put a probe on their surfaces, and use it to determine the rocks' elemental compositions, an ability that the Viking landers lacked. These rock probes yielded the single major surprise from the Pathfinder mission.

Of the first three rocks subjected to Sojourner's probe, two turned out to be basaltic, volcanic rocks of a type highly common on Earth, and just about what was expected from what we know of Mars's history. But the third rock, called "Barnacle Bill" in the playful terminology of NASA's scientists, proved to be a type of rock called andesite. Andesite appears fairly often on our planet; its name refers to the Andes in South America, where this type of rock is abundant. But they are abundant because they are produced by plate-tectonic activity. The discovery of andesite rock on the Martian surface calls for a reassessment of our views of Mars's history. No scientist believes that Mars now has plates in tectonic motion, but it does seem that Mars had not only active volcanoes in its distant past but also a process similar to the plate tectonics that produced many of the volcanic rocks on Earth.

Welcome as the Pathfinder mission has been to scientists, they are quick to admit that it has provided only a modest amount of scientific data. This comes as no surprise, since Pathfinder was planned primarily as a technological mission, to test a new method (the airbags) for landings on Mars and to develop a vehicle (Sojourner) that could explore the Martian surface, if only modestly. Intriguingly, Pathfinder produced one important result simply by using its radio to transmit photographs and other information to Earth. These streams of data allowed accurate tracking of the spacecraft's location, revealing new information about how Mars slowly and slightly changes its rotation. The changes depend on the distribution of mass inside Mars, so by following the spacecraft, astronomers could determine that Mars has a dense, metal-rich core about two thousand miles across, whose existence, formerly only suspected, has now been verified.

NASA sent another spacecraft to Mars in 1997, the Mars Global Surveyor, designed to orbit the red planet and to survey its entire surface. During late 1997 and most of 1998, Global Surveyor used the Martian atmosphere's drag on its solar panels (a technique called "aerobraking") to change its trajectory around Mars from a highly elliptical orbit into a nearly circular one, 235 miles above the Martian surface. From there, through more than 8,000 orbits that extend over a full Martian year (687 Earth days), Global Surveyor is poised to perform its observational tasks, which will be complete as the calendar turns into the year 2000.

Chief among Global Surveyor's goals is the preparation of a detailed, three-dimensional map of the entire surface of Mars. In addition to its cameras, the space-craft carries a laser rangefinder to measure the heights of Martian surface features to within a few yards. Global Surveyor also has a magnetometer to measure Mars's magnetic field—assuming that this field proves strong enough to be detected. But even if no detectable magnetic field exists now, Mars almost certainly had a significant magnetic field billions of years ago, which should have led to the formation of magnetized rocks. Global Surveyor's magnetometer will be able to measure the "remnant magnetism" of rocks beneath it, and thus discover the history of magnetism on Mars.

Still more exciting to scientists is Global Surveyor's thermal emission spectrometer, or TES, which can measure emission from Mars at infrared wavelengths that reveal the chemical composition of the emitting material. In addition, infrared emission provides an easy way to measure temperatures: A hotter object emits more infrared than a cooler one of the same size, so the TES can produce a "thermal map" of Mars. One of the great results from that map could be the discovery of underground hot springs below the Martian surface, revealed by the heat that leaks upward, as well as by the existence of higher-than-expected amounts of sulfide compounds and clay minerals above them, deposited by many years of exposure to underground spring waters. In the hunt for life on Mars, a subsurface hot spring would rank as number one among all places to search. If Global Surveyor finds anything suggestive of such a spring, that area will become the immediate prime target of future missions to our planetary neighbor.

Every 26 months, as Earth and Mars orbit the sun, their changing relative positions reach an orientation that allows the lowest-energy trajectories for spacecraft to pass between the planets. NASA now plans to send at least one spacecraft to Mars at the end of 1998 and also during each of the next three "launch windows," in 2001, 2003, and 2005. With skill, proper planning, funding, and luck, the year 2005 will bring a sample return mission, in which rocks from Mars will be brought to Earth for detailed analysis in our best laboratories.

In December 1998, NASA plans to launch Mars Surveyor, a mightier instrument than either Global Surveyor or Mars Pathfinder. Like the Vikings, Mars Surveyor will include both an orbiter, to study the planet from above and to relay data back to Earth, and a lander, which can make detailed investigations of a small area on the surface. Unlike the Vikings, however, Mars Surveyor's orbiter and lander will make separate journeys to Mars, a plan that allows NASA to use relatively inexpensive Delta II rockets for each trip. Also unlike the Vikings, Mars Surveyor's lander will aim not for the broad plains of Mars but for a spot near the edge of the south polar cap, where the lander will cut carefully into the soil, exposing successive layers whose images will be sent to Earth. During the same launch window, at the end of 1998 or the beginning of 1999, the Japanese space agency will launch the Planet-B spacecraft, which will carry a spectrometer that can make detailed measurements of Mars's atmospheric composition as it orbits the planet.

Bringing Martian Samples Back to Earth

For definitive proof of life on Mars, we probably need not just photographs or measurements of Martian rocks but actual samples of Mars, to be studied in detail in terrestrial laboratories. The analysis of ALH 84001 illustrates the impressive fineness of detail that sophisticated laboratories on Earth can achieve, with equipment to count tiny numbers of radioactive nuclei, or to perform intricate chemical analyses. NASA's plans to bring samples back from Mars with the mission sent in the year

2005 will rely on what scientists and engineers learn from previous missions, which should allow them to create ever-more-competent spacecraft.

Like the Mars Surveyor, the mission to be launched in 2001 will include an orbiter and a lander. The orbiter should carry a gamma-ray spectrometer, capable of performing a global chemical analysis of Mars with considerably higher sensitivity than that made by Global Surveyor. The orbiter will also carry infrared-observing instruments, to obtain images and make spectroscopic measurements that are likewise superior to Surveyor's capabilities. The lander will bring to the Martian surface a rover abut four times more massive, and far more capable, than Sojourner, capable of travelling not tens of yards but tens of miles across the surface, stopping at interesting sites to take photographs and make measurements. The rover should be able to identify and to "cache" the most appealing soil samples and pieces of rock, saving them at a single location for collection by a later mission to bring them to Earth.

Next, in the year 2003, NASA will launch a still more advanced mission to send a probe with a rover to Mars. Like the spacecraft launched in 2001, this mission should find and cache samples for the sample return mission, to be launched in 2005, to bring back to Earth. By sending two separate missions to collect samples to two disparate regions of Mars, we shall have a choice of which samples to return to Earth. The Mars mission to be launched in 2005 may have no exploration to perform on its own, but will instead home in on the beacon left by the cache from one of the two earlier missions, send a vehicle to the Martian surface to gather the samples, and bring them to our home planet.

The ultimate goal of the three missions of 2001, 2003, and 2005 will be the return of about two pounds of the Martian surface, less than the mass of material in the Martian meteorite ALH 84001. However, ALH 84001 represents a single chunk of the ancient Martian surface, a random sample of the material hard enough to survive being blasted from Mars before passing through interplanetary space. The two pounds of samples to be collected on Mars will include a multitude of individual samples, gathered on the Martian surface after serious examination and study by the best rovers we can produce, including "friable" (breakable) rock as well as soil samples from regions judged the most likely to yield signs of biological activity. These two pounds will have been collected from several dozen separate locations, each one identified as promising something of interest.

ALH 84001 is a "tough rock," made by volcanic activity, congealed into something like the igneous rocks of Earth. What astrobiologists really want to study are sedimentary rocks, those formed by slow deposits under water. On Earth, these are the fossil-bearing rocks; even an expert paleontologist must look for a mighty long time before finding fossils in igneous rocks. But sedimentary rocks are too fragile to reach Earth by the impact method. Any impact that blasts them will destroy them, shattering them into small bits that will not be recognizable as meteorites if they should happen to fall on Earth.

Note that if we can bring samples of Martian rock and soil back to Earth, the samples never become obsolete. In fact, as scientists develop new techniques for studying them, the samples become effectively more up-to-date, not in their date of origin but in the information we can extract from them. ALH 84001 provides a perfect example of this fact, even though it came to Earth by accident rather than human endeavor. As scientists improve their techniques for scrutinizing a meteorite such as this one, and recognize that additional tests can be made on samples they have already studied, they can draw new information from old rocks.

The Face on Mars

The Viking missions to Mars, which had been motivated in large part by the possibility of finding primitive Martian life, also stimulated a dramatic reawakening of the notion that advanced civilizations inhabit Mars. As the Viking photographs all too clearly revealed a planet hostile to life, the power of the human imagination shifted its focus toward the only slightly less exciting concept of highly advanced

Martians who had long vanished from the planet. The touchstone of this belief emerged when the Viking orbiters photographed a topographical feature that became known around the world as the Face on Mars. Relying on the fact that anyone can see a face in these features, and on NASA's stubborn refusal to acknowledge this "face" as evidence of an advanced civilization, a cottage industry sprang up to develop the hypothesis (never referred to as such) that a superior alien race must have created the 1600-foot-wide Face on Mars. According to this hypothesis, ancient Martians not only resembled humans, but also possessed the desire and ability to create an enormous face to mark their existence. In addition, NASA's refusal to see the face as a sign to return to Mars for further exploration had to imply either woeful, willful ignorance or a cover-up of Watergate proportions.

The counter-hypothesis, that the Face on Mars consists of natural rock formations in which the human brain tends to see a face, has had less emotional appeal. Despite the history of the Martian canals, and despite the repeatedly demonstrated

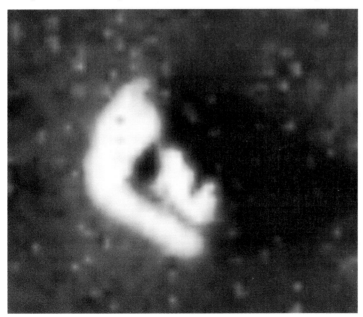

ability of our brains to see a face where none really exists (compare the Man in the Moon and the Great Stone Face in New Hampshire), the Face on Mars continued to persuade many people that civilizations must have created this giant artifact on our planetary neighbor. In April 1998, NASA, having heroically refused the opportunity to obtain

These rocks, photographed by the Viking orbiter, suggest the features of a human face.

additional funding by jumping on the Face on Mars bandwagon, finally had the Global Surveyor spacecraft in orbit around Mars, able to photograph the "face" as part of its scientific mission.

Before these photographs came back to Earth, Tobias Owen, the astronomer who had first noted that these rocky outcroppings resemble a face, predicted that the new

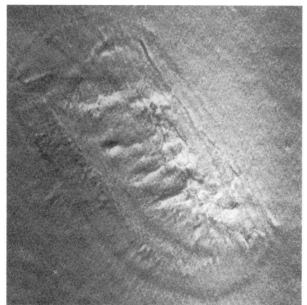

In 1988, Mars Global Surveyor photographed the Face on Mars and confirmed that it consists of natural topographic features.

images would hardly convince true believers, who would proceed to claim either that the photographs had been doctored, or that NASA had destroyed the face to avoid frightening the Earth, or that the Martians themselves had returned for this task. Owen noted that "the conspiracy theorists never challenge the authenticity of the original Viking photograph," which in fact would be far easier to have altered, since it contains so much less detail than the images from Global Surveyor. Reaction to the new images of the "face" promptly verified Owen's prediction, as competing web pages appeared to explain, somewhat confusingly, that NASA had sent nuclear weapons on an interplanetary mission to destroy the Face on Mars, or that the "face" is still quite recognizable as humanoid, despite the fact that the region now seems to be an eroded, flat-topped mesa. Happily, either the cold logic of the situation, or extreme boredom (could both be at work?) have persuaded the average citizen that the Face on Mars no longer ranks as serious evidence for a long-vanished Martian civilization. The possibility remains open that the first advanced civilization to appear on Mars will be human.

Deimos and Phobos

Two small satellites accompany Mars on its elliptical trajectory around the sun. Asaph Hall discovered Deimos (pronounced DEE-mos) and Phobos (FOE-bos) in 1877, using the then world's largest telescope, the 26-inch refractor at the U.S. Naval Observatory in Washington, DC, during one of Mars's periodic close approaches to Earth—the same close approach that led Giovanni Schiaparelli to record his observations of Martian "canali." Dark and battered hunks of rock, named for the horses that pulled the chariot of the war god Mars, Deimos and Phobos have diameters of only 8 and 15 miles, respectively.

The two Martian satellites probably began their careers as asteroids that happened to pass close to Mars. First captured by Mars's gravity into highly elongated orbits, Deimos and Phobos achieved nearly circular orbits after millions of passes through Mars's thin atmosphere. These orbits keep them only a few thousand miles above Mars's surface; Phobos, only 3,700 miles above the Martian surface, circles the planet in just under 8 hours, far less time than Mars takes to rotate. Hence an observer on Mars would see Phobos move across the sky from west to east, in movement opposite to that followed by all other celestial objects. On the other hand, Phobos and Deimos are so small that they would provide inhabitants of Mars with nothing like our moon's illumination, or the visible features of the Man in the Moon, even though Phobos and Deimos are only one-fortieth and one-sixteenth as far from Mars,

Mars's two small satellites, Phobos (bottom right) and Deimos (bottom left) appear in this photomontage with the asteroid Gaspra (top).

respectively, as the moon is from the Earth.

The Viking photographs of Deimos and Phobos show cratered and grooved surfaces, almost certainly the result of impacts made more than 4 billion years ago, during the great era of bombardment by the debris left over from the formation of the solar system. The two moons have surfaces almost as dark as any found in space, similar in color and reflectivity to what are believed to be the oldest asteroids. Because these match those of the meteorites called carbonaceous chondrites, which are thought to rank as the oldest rocks we have found, the conclusion follows that Deimos and Phobos should have a carbon-rich composition similar to that of the ancient meteorites.

Generations of spacefaring minds have imagined themselves on either Deimos or Phobos, handy platforms from which to study the Martian surface in detail. Simple calculations show that any moon only a few miles across must produce gravitational forces so weak that an astronaut could almost achieve lift-off with a good running start (not the easiest feat when dressed for space), and could certainly do so with a good bicycle and an upward-pointing ramp. If cost were no object, new Olympic sports, more exotic even than whitewater synchronized swimming, could easily be developed for the two tiny moons of Mars, where gravity would offer only a modest intrusion into an athlete's highly developed routines.

CHAPTER SEVEN

JUPITER

Of the sun's nine planets, one has so much more mass than the others that a cursory survey would describe the solar system as made of the sun and Jupiter, plus a host of lesser objects—the other planets, their satellites, asteroids, comets, and meteoroids.

With eleven times the Earth's diameter, and 318 times its mass, Jupiter could swallow more than thirteen hundred Earths, if it were hollow and had a mind to do so. In addition to its enormous size and mass, Jupiter's most significant attribute is the planet's low average density: 1.3 grams per cubic centimeter, in comparison with 5.5 for Earth and at least 3.97 for the other inner planets. This low density provides the explanation of Jupiter's great mass. As Jupiter formed, it managed to retain large

Jupiter shown in a photomontage, has 11 times Earth's diameter.

amounts of hydrogen and helium, the lightest and most abundant elements in the disk of matter that formed the planets. Unlike Jupiter, Earth and the other inner planets lost essentially all of their hydrogen and helium once the sun began to shine. As a result, those four planets are small, rocky, and dense, whereas Jupiter and the other giant planets are large and comparatively rarefied.

Jupiter succeeded in retaining hydrogen and helium because the planet formed, and continues to orbit, at 5.2 times the Earth's distance from the sun. At this distance, every square centimeter facing the sun receives a small fraction $(1/(5.2)^2$, or about 1/27) of the solar energy that falls on a sun-facing square centimeter at the Earth's distance. Further calculations, based on the fact that large objects radiate energy into space at rates proportional to the fourth power of their absolute temperatures, imply that Jupiter's absolute temperature should be about one-fourth of the Earth's, close to 75 K (minus 325 degrees Fahrenheit) instead of our 290 K (60 degrees Fahrenheit). Additional details, including the efficiency with which the planets reflect sunlight, and how large a greenhouse effect their atmospheres provide, will affect this ratio, but they do not change the basic fact that at Jupiter's distance, a planet must be cold with an absolute temperature somewhere below 100 K (minus 280 degrees Fahrenheit).

Jupiter's Internal Structure

The cold temperatures characteristic of the region where Jupiter formed allowed hydrogen and helium to linger longer, so that the protoplanet captured vast quantities of them. Success bred success: The more mass the protoplanet could acquire, the greater would be its chances of capturing still more by its increased gravitational forces. Each of the protoplanets ran a race between the increase in their masses (and thus their gravitational forces) and the tendency of the lightest elements to escape, once the sun began to produce light and heat. Earth lost this competition while Jupiter won it, with the result that Jupiter consists primarily of two elements almost entirely absent from Earth.

Jupiter does not lack the heavier, more familiar elements, such as carbon, nitrogen, oxygen, sodium, sulfur, manganese, iron, and nickel, but most of these elements have migrated to the planet's center, drawn by the gravitational forces that originally captured them to become part of the planet. Some heavy elements remain in the planet's outer layers, where they help form the compounds that provide the variegated colors in Jupiter's changing patterns. The majority, however, reside in the central core, whose existence planetary scientists have deduced from the known facts about Jupiter's mass and the scenario that they envision for the formation of the solar system. Within this core, the pressure arising from the weight of the overlying layers (or, if we prefer, the Jupiter's squeezing of itself by self-gravitation) keeps the heavy elements at pressures beyond our direct experience. No one knows what happens to a mixture of elements heavier than hydrogen and helium at pressures a million or so times higher than those at the Earth's surface, but we can easily imagine an immensely hot, dense syrup, a molasses of matter with 15 to 20 times the mass of Earth packed into a core smaller than our moon.

The bulk of Jupiter consists of hydrogen and helium, which probably contribute 99 percent of Jupiter's mass in the regions around the core. These regions are likewise tremendously affected by Jupiter's enormous self-gravitation, which compresses most of the hydrogen and helium so much that these elements become superconducting and metallic liquids. "Superconducting" means that the matter offers essentially zero resistance to electrical currents, while "metallic" implies that the matter behaves like a metal with respect to electrical and magnetic fields. The latter term can be misleading: The superconducting, metallic hydrogen and helium liquids are colorless fluids, nothing like the metal bars that the term may suggest. We are dealing here with a mighty strange type of matter, utterly unknown on Earth except for brief moments in high-pressure laboratory experiments. Jupiter has sufficient self-gravitation to make this strange matter the dominant component of its interior.

Outside the region of liquid, metallic hydrogen and helium, lower pressures allow hydrogen and helium to exist in the familiar gaseous form, though at densities much higher than we usually encounter for gases on Earth. The outermost layers of the planet—the ones we observe, and from which we must deduce the properties of the interior—consist of hydrogen and helium gas. Sunlight has a significant heating effect on these gaseous regions, just as it does on any planet's outermost layers, but in Jupiter's case, another source of heat plays an equally important role.

Jupiter has an impressive attribute for a planet: It generates as much energy by itself as it receives from the sun! This feat results in part from the slow contraction of Jupiter's heavy-element core, and also of the liquid hydrogen and helium regions that surround the core. Because this contraction arises from Jupiter's massive self-gravitation, we can say that Jupiter vaguely resembles a protostar, that is, a star in formation. Both objects squeeze themselves significantly because they contain so much mass. Since a simple rule in physics states that compression heats a gas, the slow contraction inside either Jupiter or a protostar invariably raises the objects' internal temperatures.

The similarity between the giant planet Jupiter and a protostar has led some astronomers to refer to Jupiter as a "failed star," because Jupiter generates internal heat from its gravitationally induced contraction, just as a protostar does, but this heating of the interior never raises the central temperature to the point that nuclear fusion reactions can begin, as they do in protostars. (The onset of nuclear fusion in fact marks the moment when a protostar becomes a star.)

We may note, however, that Jupiter and a protostar have important differences. Protostars consist of gas, and even though the density of matter at their centers may rise to a hundred times the density of water, as it does in the sun, nevertheless the matter there remains gaseous. Protostars have so much mass that the tremendous pressures produced by the weight of the surrounding layers heat the material at their centers to temperatures of millions of degrees. At these temperatures, collisions among atoms inevitably strip all the electrons away from any atomic nuclei, and keep both the electrons and nuclei in the interior continuously bouncing off one another as individual particles, the behavior that defines a gas. In contrast, Jupiter's interior has either a syrupy consistency (for the heavy-element core) or a liquid one (a strange liquid, to be sure), which testify to the fact that Jupiter's internal temperatures rise to "only" many thousand degrees, not to millions, because the planet has too little mass to become a star.

Jupiter's Central Heating

Jupiter's internal source of heat raises an intriguing question: Where does the boundary lie between a giant planet and a star? This issue, not so easily resolved as one might at first anticipate, becomes highly significant when we attempt to discover planets in orbit around stars other than the sun (see Chapter 12). In nuclear-fusion terms, however, the answer appears definitive, thanks to our knowledge of the conditions required for nuclei to fuse together. The dividing line appears to reside at about 80 times the mass of Jupiter (or at 8 percent of the sun's mass, since the sun has just about 1,000 times Jupiter's mass). In objects with less mass than this, nuclear fusion will never begin; with a minimum of 80 Jupiter masses, the object will fuse a small amount of deuterium (an isotope of hydrogen, with one proton and one neutron in each nucleus) in its core; and for masses greater than 10 percent of the sun's, even ordinary hydrogen nuclei (protons) will fuse, turning the object into a low-mass, low-luminosity star.

Jupiter is a long way from being a star, even though it does exhibit the slow contraction and squeezing of its inner regions that resemble what occurs in a protostar. The net heat output from Jupiter's core every second roughly equals the solar energy contribution to Jupiter's outer layers, so Jupiter represents a rare type of object, heated from its center outward and its outside inward by approximately equal amounts of energy per second.

Jupiter's Outer Layers

Like a protostar, proto-Jupiter spun more rapidly as it contracted. The proto-planet must have acquired a sizable amount of tendency to spin during its formation process, for the resultant planet has the most rapid rotation in the solar system, requiring only a few minutes less than 10 hours to spin once. As a result of its rapid spin, Jupiter's equatorial regions move at speeds of 27,000 miles per hour, in contrast to the Earth's equatorial speed of just over 1,000 miles per hour. Jupiter's gaseous outer layers react to this rapid rotation by producing intriguing, changing patterns of light-and dark-colored bands. As the bands change, Jupiter's internally-generated heating also creates rising currents of warm clouds, while cool clouds descend. In this context, "warm" and "cool" are relative terms; even the "warm" clouds have temperatures of minus 240 degrees Fahrenheit. In any case, the "warm and light goes up, cool and dark goes down" effect combines with Jupiter's rapid rotation to produce

The outer layers of Jupiter's atmosphere present a constantly changing series of complex patterns.

the variegated patterns that we see in Jupiter's outer layers. During the past quarter-century, the Pioneer, Voyager, and Galileo spacecraft obtained successively better images of these cloud

patterns, the most magnificent on any planet.

Just what causes the colors of Jupiter's clouds remains a mystery. The methane and ammonia that provide much of the atmosphere have no color whatsoever; nor do hydrogen, helium, acetylene, ethane, water vapor, carbon monoxide, or hydrogen cyanide, all of which also exist in the planet's outer layers. Jupiter's vivid coloration must arise from molecular compounds of relatively low abundance but high potency in reflecting sunlight of certain particular colors—most prominently, red, orange, and brown. Astronomers believe that sulfur- and phosphorus-based compounds are most likely to prove the culprits of Jupiter's color scheme.

The most impressive of Jupiter's cloud features—at least during the past three hundred years—has been the Great Red Spot, a cyclonelike event several times larger than the Earth, apparently first spotted by Robert Hooke toward the end of the seventeenth century. Gases within the Great Red Spot perform their own modest

whorls, taking about a week to spin once around the center as the planet performs some twenty rotations. Things would fit together nicely if the Great Red Spot proved to be a site where serious upwelling of gas occurs, but in fact spacecraft observations have found the spot to be a site of relatively tranquility, with no such upward movement discernible. The motions

Jupiter's Great Red Spot, a sort of cyclone in its upper atmosphere, covers an area several times the size of Earth.

of the gases within the Great Red Spot thus remain today just as elusive, so far as a full explanation is concerned, as its red coloration does.

Jupiter's Magnetic Field

As befits the largest planet, Jupiter has the strongest planetary magnetic field, 20,000 times stronger than Earth's. The effects produced by this field make Jupiter on occasion the most intense source of radio waves in the solar system, emitting even more radio power than the sun. (Human civilization on Earth now allows our planet to compete for this title at certain radio wavelengths, but our planet's natural radio emission falls far below Jupiter's and the sun's.)

Like Earth's, Jupiter's magnetic field arises from the motions of electrically conductive material inside the planet. Jupiter's enormous size, in conjunction with a metallic interior and the most rapid rotation of any planet, has given strength to its magnetic field, which resembles the Earth's in its configuration, with a north and south magnetic pole roughly aligned with the planet's rotation axis. Jupiter's magnetic field extends far beyond the planet's atmosphere, affecting the motions of charged particles millions of miles from the planet. Jupiter has "Van Allen belts" of charged particles that have become trapped by the magnetic field and bombard neutral particles at high velocities as they move toward Jupiter on spiral trajectories that encircle the magnetic field lines. This bombardment produces auroras high in the atmospheres of both Jupiter and the Earth: The collisions excite molecules into higher-energy configurations, allowing them to emit light when they "de-excite" into their original, lower states of energy. At levels in the atmosphere below those where the auroras arise, sudden electrical discharges produce bolts of lightning on Jupiter, much brighter than those on our planet.

The fastest-moving of the charged particles in Jupiter's Van Allen belts produce radio emission as they spiral in the magnetic field. This emission appears in bursts, whenever a large group of these high-speed particles are ejected from Jupiter's upper

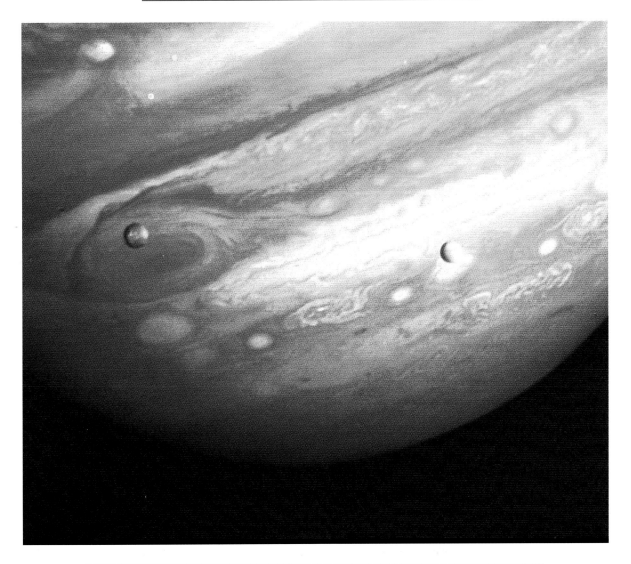

On Jupiter, the sun's largest planet, an atmospheric cyclone called the Great Red Spot is twice the size of Earth. Jupiter has four moons at least as large as Earth's own moon; two of them, Io (seen in front of the Great Red Spot) and Europa, appear in this photograph taken by the Voyager 1 spacecraft.

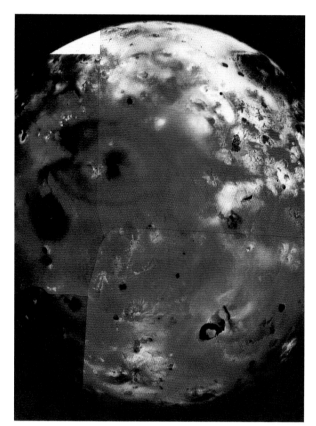

ABOVE: Ganymede, the largest planetary satellite in the solar system, has both craters and long, mountainlike ridges on its surface.

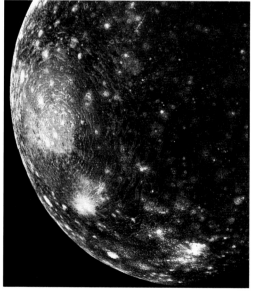

ABOVE: On Io, the innermost large moon of Jupiter, geyser-like volcanoes continually recoat the satellite's surface with sulfur-laden compounds.

RIGHT: Callisto, the outermost of Jupiter's large moons, has an icy surface, heavily cratered over billions of years.

Europa, the second of Jupiter's large moons, appears to have an icy crust that may conceal a worldwide ocean; if so, this ocean represents a prime candidate for finding microbial life in the solar system.

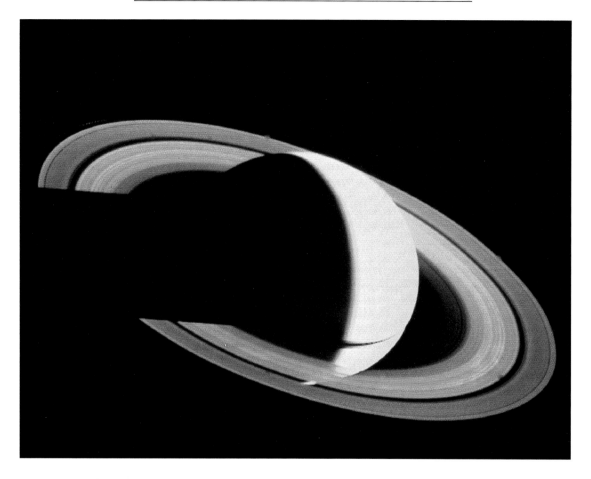

Saturn, the second-largest of the sun's family of planets, has a glorious ring system that has brought this planet its fame.

LEFT: Mercury, the sun's innermost planet, has a cratered surface much like the moon's.

BELOW: Venus, forever hiding its surface beneath a thick atmosphere, had its surface features mapped by radar systems on the Magellan spacecraft during the early 1990s.

ABOVE: Despite having just over half Earth's diameter, Mars has as much land surface as our own planet.

BELOW: Olympus Mons, the largest mountain in the solar system, is an extinct volcano that rises 15 miles above the Martian surface.

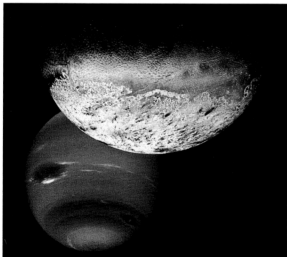

ABOVE: In 1997, the Pathfinder spacecraft landed on an ancient Martian floodplain and released its Sojourner rover to examine rocks close to the landing site.

LEFT: This montage of two images taken by the Voyager 2 spacecraft in 1989 shows the blue planet Neptune behind its large moon Triton.

While receiving a gravity boost from Earth on its way to Jupiter, the Galileo spacecraft took this photograph of South America.

atmosphere. Some of these particles also come from Io, Jupiter's innermost large satellite, where geysers continually erupt (see the following chapter). Furthermore, as Io moves through the magnetic field that surrounds Jupiter, it generates electrical currents that affect Jupiter's radio outbursts. (Some astronomers cannot resist noting that the discovery of this fact was a real "Iopener.") Were Jupiter populated by a civilization resembling our own, the "weather" forecast would have to be continually updated with a report on Io's position in the sky and the probability of severe electrical storms.

Jupiter's Rings

When the Voyager spacecraft neared Jupiter in 1979, astronomers had a key item to search for: the planet's rings. After all, they reasoned, if Saturn (and Uranus, too) have particles that form rings as they orbit the planet, why should this phenomenon not exist for Jupiter and the other giant planets as well? Of course, any such rings could hardly spread out as widely as Saturn's do, or they would have already been seen through telescopes on Earth, but surely Jupiter ought to have at least a narrow ring system, which Voyagers' cameras could detect.

The astronomers were right: Voyager 1 took a single frame that revealed a ring around Jupiter, and Voyager 2 studied the ring system far more carefully. Jupiter's rings consist of dark dust, made primarily of silicates (silicon-oxygen combinations, with mixtures of other atoms). The most significant of these rings consists of particles orbiting Jupiter at 35,000 miles above the planet's outer layers, and spans about 3,000 miles in width. Compare this with Saturn's rings, whose widths are measured in hundreds of thousands of miles, and Jupiter's rightly seem modest, but there they

Jupiter's rings, like Saturn's, consist of individual small particles orbiting the planet.

are. Astronomers eventually found rings around Neptune as well as around Jupiter, Uranus, and Saturn, closing the book of rings on the four giant planets.

Spacecraft to Jupiter

Once we knew little about Jupiter save its mass, temperature, and bandedness. The advent of the space age led to multi-year journeys into the outer solar system, made by automated spacecraft that have tremendously increased our understanding of Jupiter and the planets beyond. First to travel were Pioneers 10 and 11, which took close-up photographs of Jupiter and Saturn during the 1970s. Next came Voyagers 1 and 2, both launched in 1977, which reached Jupiter in 1979 and Saturn in 1980 and 1981. Taking advantage of a planetary line-up that occurs only once every few centuries to use a "gravitational slingshot" effect from both Jupiter and Saturn, Voyager 2 proceeded to visit Uranus in 1986 and Neptune in 1989. The Voyagers allowed us to make a complete survey of the sun's planets (if we withhold that rank from tiny Pluto), providing the basis for astronomers' judgments about the four gas giants for more than a decade. Then, after a decade and a half without any new exploration of Jupiter, the Galileo spacecraft made its way into an orbit around the largest planet as it began its mission of discovery.

To achieve its success, Galileo had to triumph over various forms of adversity that arose even before its launch, because the disaster in 1986 involving the Space Shuttle Challenger led NASA to redesign the spacecraft for additional safety. About as large and as massive as a sport utility vehicle, Galileo took six years to reach Jupiter, passing once by Venus and twice by Earth to receive "gravity boosts" from these close encounters. Galileo then sped onward, past two small asteroids, covering a total of 2.3 billion miles, more than 25 times the distance from the Earth to the sun. For a time, however, it appeared that Galileo would keep its findings private: The spacecraft's main antenna, ribbed and furled like an umbrella to survive the stress of the launch, stubbornly refused to open to its 16-foot width, despite repeated commands from the ground to unfurl, made after numerous attempts to shake or spin the space-craft in order to jar the ribs loose. Apparently the antenna's lengthy period in storage following the Challenger disaster had led to an unnoticed evaporation of the special lubricant greasing its ribs. With its main antenna unavailable, Galileo had only its much smaller, "low-gain" antenna to use for sending messages to Earth. Because this antenna could send and receive data over hundreds of millions of miles only at an extremely low rate, the entire $1.4-billion mission could transmit only 16 bits of data per second—about 1/10,000 of the rate for which Galileo was designed, and less than the speed of the most primitive modems of the 1970s!

Amazingly, the scientists and engineers involved with the Galileo project managed to work around this problem, designing new data-compression techniques and updating the receivers in the Deep Space Network system that receives signals from NASA's spacecraft. As Galileo approached Jupiter, its first task was to detach its key sub-unit, a 746-pound, aluminum-titanium probe that could (briefly!) measure pressure, temperature, and molecular composition as it descended into Jupiter's atmosphere, to be lost forever afterward. The probe was to send its results by radio to the Galileo orbiter, which contained a tape recorder that could store the data for its later, slow transmission to Earth. This tape recorder, which was and is essential for broadcasting all the photographs that Galileo might take of Jupiter's moons, had terrified the scientists during the years of Galileo's journey, for the recorder had begun (for unknown reasons) to freeze temporarily, creating fears that it might jam completely, leaving the spacecraft loaded with data but utterly unable to send any information to Earth.

The Galileo Probe Descends into Jupiter

Traveling at 100,000 miles per hour, experiencing forces of acceleration equal to 200 g (200 times the acceleration of an object falling toward the Earth's surface), the Galileo probe met Jupiter's outermost layers on December 7, 1995. Thirty miles above the visible cloud layers, where the atmospheric pressure is about half that on Earth's surface, the probe deployed a parachute to slow its fall through the rest of Jupiter's atmosphere, where it encountered wind speeds up to 350 miles per hour. Nearly an hour passed before the probe entered regions where the atmospheric pressure, more than 25 times the Earth's surface pressure, crushed the probe's electronic components and silenced it forever.

The most startling result from the Galileo probe was its measurement of an extremely low abundance of water vapor, less than one-fifth of the amount anticipated from the abundances of hydrogen and helium. However, the consensus among planetary astronomers now appears to be that the probe just happened to descend into an extremely dry region of the atmosphere, the "mother of all down-drafts," in the words of Tobias Owen of the University of Hawaii. The probe also determined that the ratio of helium to hydrogen equals 23 percent counting by mass. In the sun, this ratio equals 28 percent, so if Jupiter formed with the same helium-to-hydrogen ratio as the sun, it has lost some helium from its outer atmosphere. This suggests that in Jupiter, as in Saturn, helium slowly "rains" downward toward the planet's center. We shall examine this intriguing phenomenon more closely when we look at Saturn, where it plays a key role in heating the planet.

By mid-summer of 1996, having secured the crucial data from the probe, the Galileo team of engineers and scientists could and did exult over their triumphs, looking forward with eager anticipation to a steady stream of high-resolution images of Jupiter and its four large moons, which deserve (and get) a chapter of their own. Even though the need to use the low-gain, back-up antenna sharply reduced the total number of images that Galileo could transmit, that number totals well over a thousand. Some of the finest appear in chapter 8, which recounts what spacecraft have observed about the four good-sized worlds that orbit the sun's largest planet.

CHAPTER EIGHT

JUPITER'S SATELLITES

Giant Jupiter has an enormous retinue of satellites, a set of moons that would do any planet proud. Not so long ago, these moons seemed likely to prove barren and uninteresting, but spacecraft have revealed some of them to be arguably the most fascinating worlds in the solar system, including among them the prime spot where we may find extraterrestrial life in the solar system.

By now, astronomers have discovered 16 moons in orbit around Jupiter, and are likely to find still more. Most of these are modest hunks of rock, almost certainly asteroids that Jupiter's gravity captured into Jovian orbits long ago. Four of the moons, however, are much larger than all the others, and almost certainly formed in orbits around Jupiter, collecting matter through gravitational forces as they grew larger. These four worlds bear the collective designation of "Galilean satellites," because their existence was first recorded by Galileo Galilei in the year 1610. Primitive though Galileo's telescopes were, they easily revealed four bright objects moving in orbit around Jupiter, taking from 2 to 17 days to do so. The Galilean satellites shine so brightly that good eyesight could reveal them without a telescope—if they were removed from Jupiter's nearby glare; even so, some lynx-eyed observers have claimed to see one or more of these moons despite Jupiter's interference. Galileo sought to designate the four satellites as the "Medicean stars," no doubt as an attempt to increase his funding by the princely family of the Medici; wiser heads rejected this parochial attempt, labeling the satellites with the names of four of Jupiter's most famous lovers: Io, Europa, Ganymede, and Callisto.

For nearly three centuries, astronomers saw these and only these four objects as the moons of Jupiter. By the brightness of their reflected sunlight, Io and Europa could be judged to be about the size of Earth's moon, with Ganymede and Callisto nearly half again as large. Jupiter's family began to increase (so far as humans knowledge goes) in 1892, when the American astronomer Edward Barnard used the 36-inch reflecting telescope at Lick Observatory to discover a fifth moon, now called Amalthea, much smaller than the four Galilean satellites and orbiting inside all four of their orbits.

During the eight decades after Barnard's keen vision revealed Amalthea, improved telescopes on Earth led to the discovery of eight more moons around Jupiter. Spacecraft observations have revealed another three, bringing the current total to 16. Except for the four Galilean satellites, the largest of Jupiter's moons spans only 150

Jupiter's four large satellites are, from left to right, Io, Europa, Ganymede, and Callisto, shown in a photomontage to their correct relative sizes.

miles, like Massachusetts, while the smallest, like Chicago, measures perhaps 15 miles across. We may rightly exercise our mass-chauvinistic prejudices, waiting for further news from these modest moons before we expend much energy in caring about them.

But the four big moons demand respect. Before touring their amazingly varied surfaces, we should note that during the four and a half billion years since their formation, the inner three Galilean satellites have significantly affected one another's orbits, producing what astronomers call "orbital resonances." During the first few hundred million years after their formation, the mutual gravitational forces among these three moons slowly changed their orbits, so that today their orbital periods resonate—that is, they occur in simple multiples of one another. Io orbits Jupiter in 1.775 days; Europa takes just twice as long as Io does, or 3.55 days; and Ganymede requires twice as long as Europa, hence four times as long as Io, 7.15 days, to orbit once around Jupiter. Callisto, whose orbital period equals 16.69 days, has not yet achieved such a resonance, though it will eventually do so. As we shall see from a tour of the Jovian satellite system, these orbital resonances have important results, especially for Io, the innermost large moon.

Spacecraft Exploration of the Galilean Satellites

For three and a half centuries, astronomers could track the orbits of the Galilean satellites, but knew nothing about their appearance. Understandably, they speculated that these four moons, similar in size and all at the same distance from the sun, should likewise have similar surfaces, perhaps rocks crusted with ice. During the early 1970s, two Pioneer spacecraft sailed past Jupiter, but they obtained only poor images of the Galilean satellites. Finally, in 1979, NASA's twin spacecraft Voyager 1 and Voyager 2 each made a single pass by Jupiter and its moons, providing Earth with our first good views of these worlds. Rarely has speculation proven so pale in comparison with reality. Instead of resembling one another, the four Galilean moons turned out to differ in nearly everything but their sizes and masses, and in the fact that Jupiter's gravity has "locked on" to the denser parts of each of the moons, causing each of them to keep the same side facing Jupiter, just as the same side of our moon always faces the Earth. The Voyagers' observations of the four Galilean satellites' surfaces fueled new careers for dozens of planetary scientists, whose tenacity had to overcome a long drought of data, for no spacecraft returned to Jupiter for a decade and a half, until the Galileo mission reached Jupiter in 1995.

After surveying the planet itself through the first half of 1996, the Galileo orbiter embarked on four years of long, looping, multiweek orbits around Jupiter, each of which carried the spacecraft within a few hundred miles of either Europa, Ganymede, or Callisto. (Plans to send images from Galileo's close encounter with Io, which occurred as the spacecraft first entered the Jovian system, were abandoned once the spacecraft's high-gain antenna refused to unfurl.) Each close encounter with one of the three moons diverted Galileo into a new orbit, while simultaneously yielding several dozen high-resolution images, stored on Galileo's tape recorder for broadcast to Earth during the weeks following the event. Let us take a look at what Galileo, following on the success of the Voyager mission, has discovered about these worlds.

Io: What a Pizza!

Io, the innermost of Jupiter's large moons, bears the shortest of all astronomical names—quite long enough, however, for astronomers to argue about its pronunciation. Usually heard as EYE-oh, the satellite's name can also be pronounced EE-oh, and still other variants exist.

Io's claims to fame are sufficiently great that television newscasters have often had to wrestle with the moon's name; some of them, cutting the Gordian knot, have read this name as "ten" (explanation of this phenomenon is left to the reader).

Strangest of the Galilean satellites, Io has about the same size as our moon, with a diameter just over one-quarter of the Earth's. Also like our moon, Io consists of rock. Totally unlike our moon's, Io's surface resembles no other in the solar

In 1979 the Voyager 2 spacecraft photographed geysers on Io that eject material dozens of miles above the satellite's surface.

system. Detailed photographs by the two Voyager spacecraft revealed multicolored regions on Io, which continually change their appearance and colors. The Voyagers also discovered the explanation for these changes: Geyserlike eruptions continually recoat Io's surface with new patterns of color. The striking range of colors arises from the presence of sulfur-rich material, which can reflect primarily orange, deep red, or reddish brown light.

Two decades ago, when astronomers first perceived the eruptions on Io, the news spread that Io has active volcanoes. This fact, along with a scientist's laconic remark that "I've seen better looking pizzas," became the signature of the Voyager encounters with Jupiter. Although use of the term "volcano" for Io's eruptions hardly counts as a true error, scientists prefer to reserve the word for events that spew molten rock from reservoirs that lie many miles underground. Geysers, in contrast, blow material upward and outward from regions no more than a few hundred yards beneath the surface; this material consists primarily of liquid, not molten rock. The liquid becomes gaseous as it spews out of the ground, then condenses into solid or liquid as it falls downward. In the geysers of Yellowstone National Park, for example, superheated water from underground reservoirs periodically bursts outward as steam, some of which evaporates while the remainder falls to Earth as water.

On Io, material heated above 1,000 degrees Fahrenheit rockets outward at speeds as high 1,500 miles per hour, reaching altitudes of more than a hundred miles. On the average, a hundred thousand tons of material emerge every second from Io's subsurface layers, much of it violently, some of it in the form of gentle outflows that ooze from beneath the surface. Simple mathematics shows that in a hundred thousand years, this amount of material will coat Io's entire surface with deposits averaging more than a foot in thickness. (Of course, this does not mean that Io is growing larger: The material that coats Io comes from Io.) In a few weeks, an area on Io the size of a small state can be completely recoated by these deposits, giving it an entirely new appearance.

In addition to its liquid-belching geysers, Io does have melted rock on its surface; this rock is thoroughly mixed with sulfur compounds not found in molten lava on Earth. Lava pools such as the lake called Loki testify to the fact that Io has a source of internal heat sufficient to melt rock and to blow hot liquid, mixed with some hot ash, many miles above the moon's surface. What in the name of fire and brimstone can explain this phenomenon?

The answer was provided by an astronomer named Stanton Peale even before the Voyagers reached Jupiter and its moons. Europa and Ganymede continuously struggle with Jupiter for Io's heart and soul. Because of the orbital resonances among the three inner Galilean satellites, Io passes particularly close to Europa on every other orbit around Jupiter, and particularly close to Ganymede, the most massive of Jupiter's moons, on every fourth orbit. The gravitational pulls from Europa and Ganymede then "forbid" Io's orbit from ever becoming completely circular; instead, the orbit remains forever slightly elliptical.

This noncircularity produces a subtle but crucial effect inside Io. At any point along Io's orbit, Jupiter raises tides inside Io, making the moon bulge both toward and away from the planet. Because Io has a noncircular orbit, its velocity in orbit changes continuously as its distance from Jupiter changes. The orbital velocity changes make Io's tidal bulge oscillate back and forth through Io's interior, making the interior flex and bend. This flexing heats Io's innards through friction and raises the temperature to the point that rock near Io's surface can melt and geysers erupt on Io's surface. Io's outbursts thus draw their power from the interplay of the gravitational forces that Jupiter, Europa, and Ganymede exert—testimony to what can happen in a system with several massive objects, each of which pulls on all the others. If Earth possessed a second moon, with an orbital period locked in resonance with that of our existing satellite, our moon might likewise undergo tidal flexing that could produce erupting geysers and an ever-changing surface. How pallid a single-moon situation can be!

Like Io, Europa and Ganymede also experience tidal flexing as the result of their orbital resonances with the other two satellites. The heating produced by this process falls far below the amount on Io, however, because these moons are farther from Jupiter, which therefore produces only relatively small tidal bulges. The heating caused by tidal flexing of a satellite decreases approximately in proportion to the seventh power of the moon's distance from Jupiter, so an increase by a factor of two in distance will decrease the heating by more than a hundred times. Europa orbits Jupiter at a distance 50 percent greater than Io's, while Ganymede is almost two and a half times as far as Io from the giant planet. As a result, Io undergoes far more heating from tidal flexing than either of these other two moons. Nevertheless, tidal flexing may play a significant role on the second of Jupiter's Galilean satellites, Europa.

Europa, the Darling in the Hunt for Life

Europa has about the same size as Io and our own satellite. But in utter contrast to Io and our moon, Europa has a surface that has startled and entranced astronomers ever since they first suspected its nature. This surface—more precisely, what may lie beneath the surface—has made Europa the current favorite object for those who dream of finding living creatures on worlds beyond the Earth.

Two decades ago, when the Voyager spacecraft sailed past the Jovian system, it sent images to Earth that showed the pale, highly reflective surface of Europa, crisscrossed by long, thin, dark lines. Astronomers promptly drew the straightforward conclusion that Europa's surface is covered by ice—familiar H_2O, frozen solid at temperatures well below those in the Earth's polar regions. Water molecules certainly exist in abundance in the outer solar system, and the temperatures at five times the Earth's distance from the sun imply that water should be well frozen. On Io, to be sure, the continuing volcanic activity prevents the existence of ice; on Europa, which undergoes far less heating from tidal stress than Io does, the temperature is right for ice.

By itself, ice hardly suggests the presence of life. The satellite's power to excite derives from the conclusion that beneath its icy surface, Europa possesses a world-wide ocean. If this is so, then Europa fulfills the primary requirement that scientists envision for life to exist: the presence of liquid lakes or oceans, preferably made of water, though liquids such as ethane or methyl alcohol might also serve the purpose. Life arises, according to the modern scenario, when molecules float and interact gently, creating new and more complex types of molecules. The unchanging lattices of solids, and the low densities of gases, offer far less opportunity for these interactions than does the dense, but not too dense, fluidity of a liquid. If—and it is high time to stress this "if"—Europa has an ocean beneath its surface, that ocean represents by far the likeliest spot to find extraterrestrial life in the solar system. This raises two immediate questions: Why do astronomers believe that an ocean lies beneath the ice? And how could we investigate such an ocean, assuming that it exists?

The argument for a worldwide ocean on Europa consists of the possibility that such an ocean could exist, the result of Europa's tidal heating, and on the images of Europa sent to Earth by the Galileo spacecraft during the past few years. The possibility seems well established: Europa flexes itself in response to the tides raised by Jupiter, Io, and Ganymede, the third Galilean satellite. This flexing heats Europa's interior, not so much as Io's, but enough to maintain liquid water, provided that a layer of ice shields that water to slow the rate at which it radiates heat into space.

This possibility has grown far more likely to be reality, though it is still far from being proven so, as our view of Europa's surface has improved. After surveying Jupiter itself in 1995 and 1996, the Galileo spacecraft embarked on a series of trajectories that took it successively and repeatedly past Jupiter's large moons. Functioning brilliantly despite the technological difficulties described in Chapter 7, Galileo revealed the surfaces of these moons in stunning detail, showing features on some images that are only a few hundred yards wide. These images verify the overall impression provided by the Voyagers: Europa's surface can best be described as ice, with only a small number of impact craters on the ice. Since impacts occur regularly on the four large satellites (as we shall see in spades when we come to Ganymede and Callisto), the lack of impact craters implies that the crust has periodically melted and then refrozen, eliminating the visible traces of old craters.

Most significant of all, the Galileo images show that Europa's surface in many ways resembles the Antarctic ice pack on Earth. Long, dark bands run through the ice, often for hundreds of miles, while portions of the surface seem to be "ice rafts" that slowly change their relative positions, as if they were breaking off from larger ice floes; on occasion, these ice rafts run over one another. The long, dark bands often have a double or triple structure, like a superhighway with fast and slow lanes, suggesting that distinct regions of ice have broken apart, refrozen into a new position, and then broken apart again once or twice. Astronomers agree that these patterns match what would be expected from ice floating on liquid water, though they disagree on just how confident we should be that this water does exist. They disagree even more strongly (in a purely scientific way, of course) over the thickness of Europa's icy crust and the depth of its putative oceans. The crust might be only a few yards thick, or as much as half a mile or more; the worldwide sea might range in depth from a few hundred yards up to a few miles, like the oceans of Earth.

Europa's surface apparently consists of ice floes that slowly change their orientation with respect to one another.

The prospect of life beneath an icy layer resonates nicely with a key fact about the regions surrounding Jupiter: They teem with dangerous radiation. As we have seen, Jupiter's magnetic field traps charged particles whose interactions produce high-energy photons. Any visitors to the regions surrounding Jupiter will have to carry shielding against this radiation, and any form of life that "hoped" to evolve in this area likewise must have developed protection against x-ray and gamma-ray photons. In the case of Europa, this protection may have been automatic, provided by a thick layer of ice above the liquid seas.

In 1997, Galileo's spectroscopic observations revealed organic (carbon-containing) matter and mineral salts at the edges of some of Europa's ice cracks. Although hardly definitive proof of conditions favorable to life, this discovery added to the intensity with which planetary astronomers dream of probing the icy crust of Europa and diving into the presumed waters below. Even if Europa turned out to have an ocean so thin that it more closely resembles a huge underground lake—something like the water in Lake Vostok, which lies more than two miles beneath the icy surface of Antarctica—that water would still be a marvelous cosmic laboratory, a place where conditions favor the origin and evolution of life, if life really does arise form the proper mixture of cosmic elements, given a chance to float and to interact. Astrobiologists salivate with glee at the prospect of discovering what has happened during the past 4 billion years on another world with water. But how do we get there to find out?

As far as human astronauts go—well, not that far. First comes Mars, only later Jupiter, which has a distance several times the distance to Mars. The difficulties of supporting astronauts on a multi-year journey to the Jovian system would be matched by the difficulties of landing on Europa and drilling through the ice. Return to Earth poses another set of problems, perhaps to be overcome on a volunteer basis; nevertheless, the obstacles remain immense, a challenge that may be met by the end of the next century, but probably not during the lifetimes of this book's readers. In contrast, automated probes to Europa seem feasible for the second decade of the new millennium—if we care to invest the money and effort to send them.

Astronomers envision a number of ways to investigate what lies beneath Europa's icy surface. The simplest would be the standard method: Send a spacecraft to orbit the object, studying its surface with an array of telescopes, spectrometers, and other instruments than can provide clues to the nature of the surface and the subsurface layers. Fine though this effort would be, it could never tell us whether Europa has life beneath the ice (unless, of course, that life ran up a flag to salute us). To probe through the ice, we have two choices: We can bomb Europa, or we can puncture it.

The bombing notion is simple and cost-effective, because it is far easier to orbit Europa than to land on it. One spacecraft could drop an explosive charge that would blast through Europa's ice, and a following spacecraft could analyze the debris ejected by the explosion. If Europa does have a subsurface ocean, the contents of that ocean could be revealed by this method, though it would produce a negative reaction among some citizens of Earth (and, to be lighthearted, of Europa as well). The more natural, more expensive approach would be to design and to build a spacecraft that can first orbit Europa to study it globally, then land on the ice and deploy a drill bit (or, perhaps, a probe heated by radioactive elements) to pierce the ice and reach down to whatever currently unknown depth would suffice to emerge beneath the ice. If that depth were, for instance, a mile, we could forget about sending a drilling rig; the radioactive melter would then seem far more effective, presuming that we could launch it safely from Earth.

Because of the possibility of oceans and life on Europa, this modest moon will remain at the forefront of humanity's solar-system exploration plans for decades to come. Each of us, acting in our civic capacities, must help our leaders to decide just how much weight to lend to the search for life on Jupiter's second large moon. May we all exercise our responsibilities wisely, for if we do not, who will?

Ganymede, Lord of the Moons

The two innermost of Jupiter's four Galilean satellites, Io and Europa, turn out to have the greatest appeal—Io for its amazing, active surface and subsurface, Europa for its still more tantalizing, possible worldwide ocean. Ganymede, the third of the Galilean moons, bears the name of Jupiter's most famous male lover, and ranks as the largest satellite in the solar system. With a diameter 50 percent larger than our own

Ganymede has dark, heavily cratered terrain, as well as lighter regions altered by geological activity.

moon, Ganymede has a volume more than three times the moon's. If the two satellites had the same density of matter (mass per unit volume), Ganymede would therefore have more than three times the moon's mass, but in fact Ganymede has only twice the mass of the moon. The conclusion follows that unlike our moon, and unlike Io and Europa, Ganymede's interior must contain large amounts of low-density material mixed with the rock. That low-density material can only be ice; no other simple molecules will freeze at the temperatures characteristic of Jupiter and its moons to produce anything with a density comparable to our familiar ice.

Thus even though Ganymede has a size comparable to Mercury's, its low density gives it a mass only 45 percent of Mercury's. Since Callisto, the outermost Galilean satellite, has a density comparable to Ganymede's, it too must consist of an ice-and-rock mixture, with the two components present in roughly equal amounts. The four large moons thus vaguely duplicate the solar system: Two smaller, rocky objects orbit relatively close to Jupiter, while two larger, rock-and-ice moons, which apparently retained more low-density matter as they formed, circle the planet at greater distances.

Ganymede has an unusual surface—not so startling as Io's or Europa's, but highly remarkable nonetheless. That surface consists of light and dark regions, each covering about half the total. Though impact craters dot the entire surface, they concentrate in the darker regions. This immediately suggests that the lighter regions are younger, and formed after the solar system's era of intense bombardment had ended. Most striking of all Ganymede's features are the parallel ridges and valleys of the lighter regions, whose contours resemble, in both their sizes and shapes, the sinuous terrain of the Appalachian mountains in the eastern United States.

From the way that the surface reflects sunlight, we know that both the light and dark regions are rich in ice. This ties in nicely with the conclusion that ice forms half of Ganymede's interior, and suggests an explanation for the ridgelike aspect of the lighter regions. Picture Ganymede as it was four and a half billion years ago, an aggregate of rock together with an ice-and-water slush. Ongoing bombardment might have continually melted the surface, allowing the heaviest elements to sink toward the center. Then, as the era of bombardment came to an end, the surface finally froze for good, perhaps not in a single slow, smooth process, but rather in episodic events that saw freezing occur at different times below different parts of the satellite's surface. Since water expands as it freezes, these freezing events could have buckled the surface, with each separate ridge-and-valley terrain formed by a single event.

Ganymede has another claim to fame besides its size: by far the strongest magnetic field of any moon in the solar system. Scientists remain baffled, at least to a large extent, when challenged to explain how planets and moons acquire a magnetic field. They do, however, agree on one requirement: To maintain magnetism, a planet or satellite must have an iron-rich core. Mercury and the Earth are known (by deduction) to possess such a core; Venus and Mars presumably have much smaller cores, perhaps less rich in iron and nickel. Deep beneath the rock and ice that fill most of its volume, Ganymede apparently has an iron-rich core something like the Earth's, in which electrical currents generate a magnetic field.

Given its size, solid surface, and richness of terrain, we may conclude that if Ganymede had an atmosphere that could trap significant amount of solar heat, it might be ripe for colonization. (One of the great science-fiction novels of the 1950s, Robert Heinlein's *Farmer in the Sky*, imagines just this situation.) As things stand in reality, even a large, solid world poses serious real-estate sales difficulties, orbiting as it does at a location five times farther from the sun than our home planet. Since Mars has a more clement climate and a larger surface area than Ganymede, those of us who shudder at the prospect of what humans will do to revamp the solar system's terrains may take some comfort by reflecting that first comes Mars, only later Ganymede.

Callisto Gets No Respect

When the public considers the four Galilean satellites of Jupiter, it pays the least attention to Callisto (kah-LISS-toe), the outermost of them. Io has geysers; Europa has ice and possible oceans with life; Ganymede is the largest moon in the solar system and has a terrestrial range of geological features. What can Callisto claim? Only the most densely cratered surface in the solar system.

The Voyager mission found what Galileo has confirmed: Callisto has a worldwide landscape of craters, more craters, and craters on top of craters. Some regions on the moon and Mercury can rival Callisto in crater density, but on Callisto the craters just keep on going. Because Callisto, like Ganymede, has a relatively low average density (1.9 grams per cubic centimeter, compared to the 3 or so grams per cubic centimeter that rock provides), we may conclude that like Ganymede, Callisto has large amounts of ice mixed in with its rock. The presence of this ice, which is confirmed by spectroscopic studies of sunlight reflected by Callisto, makes Callisto's surface different from the moon's and Mercury's. On the latter two, the craters have bowl-like shapes, which we expect would arise from the impacts of fast-moving objects on a rocky surface. But Callisto's craters have much flatter bottoms. This fits with the notion that

Callisto's surface contains large amounts of ice mixed with the rock. At the extremely low temperatures on Callisto (about minus 250 to minus 300 degrees Fahrenheit), ice cannot remain rigid for millions and billions of years; instead, it slowly slumps, so that the up-and-down relief gradually flattens out.

The existence of an ice-rich surface on Callisto also explains why this moon has no craters larger than a few dozen miles across, and in particular no large impact basins like those on Mercury and the moon. Enormously large features are the first to subside in a material that behaves like a fluid, even though it may take millions of years to mimic what a fluid achieves in a second. Callisto does have a few large bulls-

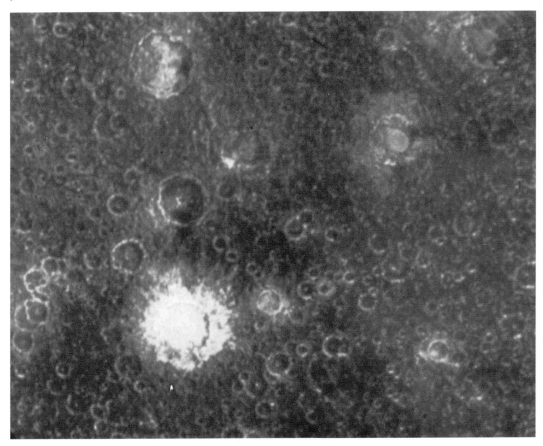

Callisto has an icy, heavily cratered surface.

eye patterns, something like giant, concentric, frozen waves, that may well be the remains of ancient impact basins. We know that impacts are still occurring on Callisto, because we can see a few fresh craters, marked as such by rims that are much brighter than the others. These new impacts have exposed fresh ice that reflects light more effectively than does the old ice, which has weathered through hundreds of millions or billions of years.

Phrases such as the last one emphasize the enormous differences in time scales that we encounter in a tour of the solar system, or even of Jupiter's large moons. On Ganymede and Callisto, little has changed, or will change, during periods of time measured in billions of years. On Io and Europa, however, we see changes occur from week to week, and probably even more rapidly if we had the capability of observing on these far shorter time scales. The difference arises from within the satellites: Io and Europa continuously experience significant heating through tidal flexing, while Ganymede and Callisto do not. As a result, Ganymede and Callisto may be uncharitably called boring worlds, large though they may be in comparison with our moon and with Jupiter's two inner, more changeable Galilean satellites.

If Jupiter were the outermost of the sun's planets, we could hardly complain that the solar system lacks variety. In fact, however, three other giant planets orbit the sun, surrounded myriad icy objects, some of the debris from the process that formed the planets. Of the planets beyond Jupiter, one has gained fame as the ringed planet. To reach this fabled world, present in every cartoon that depicts our cosmic setting, we must sail on to realms of space at nearly twice Jupiter's, and 10 times the Earth's, distance from the sun. There in the frigid darkness, mighty Saturn and its retinue reflect some dim sunlight our way.

SATURN AND ITS MOONS

Saturn, Jupiter's only planetary size rival, has had better press than Jupiter since 1659, when the Dutch astronomer Christiaan Huygens saw a broad ring system surrounding its equator. Generations of astronomy innocents, who can neither identify Saturn on the sky nor describe its size, its composition, or what its rings are made of, can easily reproduce the pattern that Huygens drew 340 years ago, a tribute to the totemic power of a planet with a ring. People may not know much about astronomy, but everyone knows that planets ought to look like Saturn.

The Planet That Floats

Saturn has a diameter nine times the Earth's, not much less than Jupiter's eleven times. In mass, however, Saturn falls far short of Jupiter, with 95 times the Earth's mass to Jupiter's 318. Saturn's relatively large volume and low mass imply an impressively low density, barely two-thirds of the density of water. In fact, Saturn's average density of 0.68 grams per cubic centimeter, just over half of Jupiter's, gives the ringed planet by far the lowest density of any giant planet. Put Saturn in a giant ocean and it will float higher than any iceberg, because ice has a density of 0.92 grams per cubic centimeter and keeps only 8 percent of its volume above the surface.

Of course, no ocean that we know could hold Saturn. The planet "floats" through interplanetary space, governed in its motion not by the buoyant force of a liquid but by the sun's gravitational attraction. At 9.5 times the Earth's distance from the sun, Saturn takes 29 $^1/_2$ years to complete each orbit, passing 2 $^1/_2$ years in each of the 12 constellations of the zodiac. As the slowest-moving planet known to ancient cultures, Saturn seemed the elder statesman among the objects that wandered over the dome of heaven. Today we know that Saturn's majestic pace derives from the planet's great distance from the sun; we have also discovered far more distant objects, which take much longer to make each trip around our star.

A Pale Imitation

Except for Saturn's great ring system, we can describe the sun's sixth planet as a pale—in all senses of the word—copy of Jupiter. Like Jupiter, most of Saturn consists of liquid hydrogen and helium, which surrounds a dense, solid core made of heavier elements. Saturn's outermost layers are mainly gaseous hydrogen and helium, along with methane and ammonia, which are the simplest molecular compounds that

Saturn, with nine times the diameter of Earth, has a density much less than the density of water.

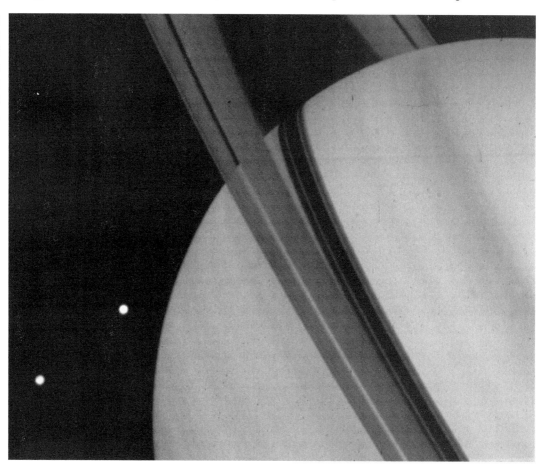

hydrogen forms with carbon and nitrogen atoms. Because Saturn has less of the molecular compounds that give Jupiter its pronounced coloration, the sunlight that Saturn reflects shows pale shades of lemon yellow, yellow-orange, brown, and white. Saturn's whitish clouds owe their hue largely to the presence of ammonia molecules, while the origin of its pale colors remains a mystery, as is true for the colors of Jupiter's clouds.

Saturn rotates rapidly, taking just 10 $^1/_2$ hours to spin once, about 25 minutes longer than Jupiter does. This rapid rotation helps drive strong wind currents that create changing patterns at the top of Saturn's atmosphere, with noticeable color contrasts where the different wind currents meet—like Jupiter's, but milder. Because Saturn has a weaker magnetic field than Jupiter, the planet produces less radio emission from its immediate surroundings than Jupiter does. Saturn's magnetic field leads to the production of auroral displays, but these are far less vivid than the auroras seen on Jupiter. Without being too harsh on the planet, we might say that Saturn is fortunate, from a public relations viewpoint, to possess its system of rings, as well as its fascinating veiled moon, Titan. Without these accessories, Saturn would appeal to us no more than Uranus does.

Hard Rain Falling

The most exciting fact about Saturn as a planet lies inside the mass of liquid hydrogen and helium that fills most of Saturn's interior. There, for thousands upon thousands of miles, a rain of liquid-helium droplets is falling. These falling droplets continuously warm the planet by impacts with the material through which they fall.

Helium rain falls through Saturn because the planet's internal blender works with less than optimum efficiency. If Saturn's interior were perfectly mixed, every small volume within its liquid region would contain the same proportions of hydrogen and helium. This perfection would arise if Saturn's interior could maintain higher pressures and temperatures than the actual values. As things are, however, droplets of helium tend to form in Saturn's liquid interior, like the droplets that appear in a chef's sauce that ceases to stay well mixed as it cools. Because the helium droplets are denser than the rest of the hydrogen-helium mixture, Saturn's gravity pulls them toward the planet's center. Droplets are therefore always raining inward through Saturn, heating the hydrogen-and-helium liquid by impacts as they do so. The energy from helium rainfall makes a sizable contribution to Saturn's total heat budget, most of which comes from a familiar source, the radiation received from the distant sun. Because Saturn is much less massive than Jupiter, it does not undergo the slow contraction, induced by self-gravitation, that heats Jupiter's interior.   Instead, to warm itself, Saturn must rely on the helium rain that falls through its liquid interior. Jupiter has its own helium rainfall, but it contributes far less heating to the planet than does the contraction of Jupiter's interior.

This helium that rains through Saturn travels relatively slowly, and, at any given time, only a tiny fraction of the total amount of helium inside Saturn has condensed into droplets of helium rain. But once these helium droplets have fallen into the core, they will remain there. Sooner or later (in fact, much later), almost all of Saturn's helium will have condensed into droplets and fallen through the liquid. Astronomers' understanding of the interiors of Jupiter and Saturn relies primarily on their theoretical understanding of how large objects, made mostly of hydrogen and helium, will behave. However, the concept of helium rain inside Saturn does have a key piece of evidence to support it. Spectroscopic observations of Saturn's outer layers reveal that those layers contain only 3 helium atoms for every 100 hydrogen atoms. Since Jupiter's outer layers have a helium-to-hydrogen ratio more than twice as large, while the sun has a ratio of 9.7 to 100, the conclusion seems reasonable that the liquid region inside Saturn has already lost much of its helium in the mundane rain it never can regain.

The Rings of Saturn

Majestic rings surround the sun's sixth planet. Though we now know that all four giant planets have ring systems, Saturn's stand out dramatically, for they extend to distances three times the planet's diameter, instead of being tightly confined within a narrow band of orbits, like the rings of Jupiter, Uranus, and Neptune. A trip from one side to the other of Saturn's rings covers a distance three-quarters of the distance from the Earth to the moon.

Since the mid-nineteenth century, astronomers have known that Saturn's rings consist of billions of particles, some as large as a house, most no larger than grains of sand. Each of these particles amounts to a miniature satellite of Saturn—a moon that modern observations have shown to be mainly made of ice. If all these ring particles were clumped together, they would create only a small moon, a satellite that can never form because Saturn's tidal forces forever keep the ring particles from coalescing into a single object close to the planet. The particles might once have belonged to a moon that moved closer to Saturn and was disrupted by tidal forces, or they might only have attempted to form a moon and found themselves prevented from doing so.

Nearly all of the particles in the rings move in circular orbits around Saturn, for if any one of them did not, the combined gravitational forces from all the other particles would quickly circularize the renegade's orbit. Astronomers are fond of noting that Saturn's rings are the thinnest object known in comparison to their width, and will take further delight in explaining why this is so. Once again, gravity does the trick. If one of the ring particles happens to rise a bit above, or to fall a bit below, the plane of the rings, the gravitational forces from the other particles attract it back into the orbital plane containing them. Thus even though Saturn exerts the dominant gravitational force on each of the ring particles, their combined force does affect the particles' mutual orientation and keeps the rings so thin that a journey from the top to the bottom of the ring system covers less than 100 feet! If a page of this book represents the thickness of Saturn's rings, the page must be half a mile wide to model their width.

The Voyager spacecraft's photos of Saturn's rings show gaps where relatively few particles orbit the planet.

In addition to maintaining the rings as a thin system of particles moving in circular orbits, gravitational forces among the ring particles also produce changing, spokelike features, first photographed in detail by the two Voyager spacecraft that passed by Saturn in 1980 and 1981. Much more noticeable than these subtle features are gaps in the rings: Certain distances from the planet are characterized by a near total absence of any orbiting particles. The most prominent of these gaps, named after the astronomers who first observed them, are the Cassini Division, about 37,000 miles above Saturn's outer layers, and the Encke Division, about 20 percent farther from Saturn's cloud tops. Ten times wider and far more noticeable than the Encke Division, the Cassini Division spans

more than 2,000 miles, and can be easily seen with even a modest telescope.

These gaps in the rings arise not from the mutual gravitational attractions among the ring particles, but rather from the perturbing effects of Saturn's inner satellites. The Cassini Division arises from the effects of the gravitational forces from Saturn's innermost sizable moon, Mimas (pronounced either MEE-muss or MYE-muss). Mimas's orbital period equals exactly twice the period of any particle orbiting Saturn at the distance of the Cassini Division. This means that on every second orbit around Saturn, any such particle would find itself tugged outward by Mimas. Though modest, this tugging works in "resonance"; that is, its effects are cumulative. Mimas has therefore managed to clear a gap of a thousand miles on either side of its one-to-two orbital resonance, so the rings contain much smaller numbers of particles whose orbital periods are half of Mimas's than of particles whose orbital periods are a bit larger or smaller than this value. The clearing has not proven completely efficient, however: Voyager's close-up photographs revealed significant numbers of particles within the Cassini Division.

As they orbit, some of Saturn's ring particles are strongly affected by the gravitational forces from satellites close to them, called shepherd satellites. In 1979, the Pioneer spacecraft discovered Saturn's outermost ring, far more confined in width than the broad rings we know so well. This "F ring" owes its existence to two shepherd satellites, Pandora and Prometheus, which the Voyager spacecraft first saw in 1980. These moons produce separate strands within the F ring and lace those strands into intricate braids, each of which consists of millions of tiny particles that orbit Saturn while responding to the modest tugs from their shepherds.

Saturn's Moons

Unlike the sun's other planets, Saturn has moons in all size categories: huge, medium, modest, and tiny. Saturn's largest moon, Titan, has almost the same size as Ganymede; its four medium-size moons (Rhea, Iapetus, Dione, and Tethys) have diameters of 650 to 940 miles; eight smaller moons (Enceladus, Mimas, Hyperion, Phoebe, Janus, Epimetheus, Prometheus, and Pandora, ranked in decreasing order of size) span from 55 to 310 miles; and at least five tiny moons (Helene, Atlas, Calypso, Telesto, and Pan) are known, with diameters of 10 to 20 miles. Only a moon expert can know and love all these satellites, whose number will surely increase as we survey Saturn more closely—and to which a tidy mind must already add the billions of moonlets that collectively form Saturn's rings. We can simplify matters considerably by stating that of Saturn's 18 known moons, only two have a vivid claim to our attention: Titan the giant and Iapetus the oddball.

TITAN

Titan, 3,200 miles in diameter, is one of the big six moons in the outer solar system, competing with Jupiter's four Galilean satellites and Neptune's large moon, Triton, for the size prize, which Titan loses by only a hair (70 miles) to Ganymede. Like Ganymede and Callisto, Titan has a rocky core, surrounded by layers of ice. Indeed, Saturn's giant satellite may turn out to look much like those two moons of Jupiter. But we have never seen Titan's surface.

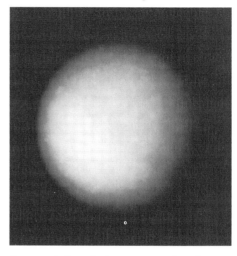

Titan, the largest moon of Saturn, keeps its surface hidden from view beneath its thick, opaque atmosphere.

Saturn's largest moon remains a shrouded mystery, for its thick atmosphere constantly conceals its surface, an attribute that makes Titan unique among all the moons of the solar system. Titan's atmosphere, like the Earth's, consists mainly of nitrogen molecules. If this were the full story, Titan would present no mystery, because nitrogen gas is completely transparent. But a layer of organic haze high in Titan's atmosphere hides the largest area in the solar system that has never been seen by human eyes. This statement may seem ripe for contradiction. It is true that we have observed fully half of Mercury, and all of Pluto, only with Earth-bound telescopes that barely show blotchy surface markings. But Titan has more than four times Pluto's diameter, and since it is a trifle larger than Mercury, the half of Mercury never photographed by Mariner 10 covers less than half the area of Titan's never-seen surface.

In comparison with our own air, Titan's atmosphere rises to great heights, because the satellite's gravitational force is far less than Earth's. But what counts (at least to us surface dwellers) is how much pressure the atmosphere exerts at the surface, and here Titan surpasses Earth, with a pressure 50 percent greater than the pressure we feel at the Earth's surface. This means that Titan's atmosphere produces 200 times the surface pressure on Mars. If we rank objects in the solar system by their atmospheric surface pressures (a competition that requires possession of a solid surface), Venus comes first, then Titan, then Earth, then Mars, with the others simply nowhere.

In addition to its dominant nitrogen component, Titan's atmosphere contains methane, argon, carbon monoxide, carbon dioxide, hydrogen cyanide, and hydrocarbons such as ethane, propane, and ethylene. In 1998, astronomers verified that the atmosphere also includes small amounts of water vapor. The haze that makes Titan's air opaque is a trace constituent floating high in the atmosphere, a sort of photochemical smog, produced by the interaction of sunlight with organic molecules, including hydrogen cyanide. These molecules link together, when sunlight strikes them, to form long-chain molecules that eventually rain onto the surface; as they do so, sunlight continuously forms new molecules to replace them, so Titan maintains its veil of smog for billions of years on end. The smog must reduce the illumination on the surface to much lower levels than Earth experiences, since the sun shines only dimly at Titan's distance to begin with. Nevertheless, life may exist beneath Titan's atmosphere.

How can we make such a bald assertion given the fact that Titan's surface temperature never varies far from 310 degrees below zero Fahrenheit? Doesn't life require liquids? Not so fast, comes the astronomical reply. On Titan we may indeed find rivers and lakes, rain storms and cataracts, just not made from water. At the temperatures and pressures on Titan's surface, ethane (C_2H_6) can behave the way that water does on our planet, furnishing the liquid for a flammable landscape, where ethane rivulets flow into ethane seas.

As we discuss more fully in Chapter 13, pools of liquid seem a prime requirement for life to begin. Thus Titan may provide one of the few places in the solar system fit for life—in this case, life that uses ethane in much the same way that Earth life uses water. Organic molecules might have formed—or might still be forming—high in Titan's atmosphere, with carbon atoms furnishing the key to binding atoms into groups. These organic molecules might rain onto the surface and into the lakes of Titan. Could primitive forms of life be floating in those lakes, awaiting our discovery? This question stimulates the juices of astrobiologists, who dream of someday floating a research vessel on Titanian lakes, testing the ethane for signs of life.

Even if no life exists on Titan, it still provides a marvelous natural laboratory. The chemical reactions that now occur on Titan mimic, in a low-temperature way, the kinds of reactions on our planet, billions of years ago, that led to the origin and development of life. Four billion years ago, Earth was rich in compounds such as methane and ammonia, which eventually disappeared as oxygen atoms combined with the ammonia (and with all the other compounds made from carbon and hydrogen) to form carbon-dioxide molecules. By studying Titan today, we can hope to learn much more about the Earth in the era when life began.

Iapetus

Iapetus (pronounced YAH-p'tuss), which almost ties with Rhea as Saturn's second largest satellite, is by far the oddest of the planet's 18 known moons. Like Rhea and the other sizable moons, Iapetus has a density that implies a primarily icy composition, with plenty of rock in addition. What stamps Iapetus as an utter oddball is its two-faced nature: This moon has a bright side, covered in ice, and an amazingly dark side, less reflective than any asphalt. Since other satellites likewise have icy surfaces, it is Iapetus's dark side that makes it unique. The best guesses about the nature of this dark coating assign it a composition similar to that of the oldest and most primitive meteorites, which are rich in carbon compounds that reflect less than 5 percent of the sunlight that hits them.

Where did this dark material come from? Like Saturn's other moons, Iapetus always keeps the same side oriented toward Saturn as it moves in orbit, but the dark side is neither this nor the hemisphere that points away from Saturn. Instead, Iapetus's dark side is the half of the moon that faces forward as the satellite orbits. Some process has coated this hemisphere with material darker than tar. Because the dark half is the forward-facing half, we may draw the inference that the source was external to Iapetus, which picked up the dark material as it orbited Saturn.

The likeliest source of the dark stuff appears to be the next moon outward, Phoebe. We can imagine something causing matter to spurt from Phoebe's surface and slowly spiral in toward Saturn, ripe for the Iapetus snowplow. But Phoebe's surface, though dark, is not as dark as the dark side of Iapetus, and has a color different from the coloration (such as it is) on that dark side. Something is amiss with astronomers' explanations, and not for the first time either. Unperturbed, the astronomers reply, "Wait for a few years and we'll take a closer look with better instruments."

Iapetus has a surface divided into highly reflective and amazingly dark regions.

The Cassini Mission to Saturn

For those who seek more knowledge of Saturn and its moons, NASA has a reward: the Cassini-Huygens mission, launched in October 1997 and scheduled to reach Saturn six and three-quarter years later, on July 1, 2004, after receiving gravity boosts from Venus in 1998, from Venus and Earth in 1999, and from Jupiter in December 2000.

The Cassini mission consists of two parts, an orbiter and a probe, analogous to those carried by the Galileo mission, which reached Jupiter in 1995. Upon the mission's arrival at Saturn, the Huygens probe will detach itself from the Cassini space-craft and descend not into Saturn, which we may assume resembles Jupiter, but onto the never-seen surface of Titan. The spacecraft will go into orbit around Saturn, spending half a dozen years in securing wide-angle and high-resolution images of Saturn, its moons, and its rings, and using its infrared, visible-light, and ultraviolet spectrometers to determine the chemical composition of the planet and its satellites. In addition, the Cassini orbiter carries a radar system to probe through the clouds of Titan, and to bounce radar waves off the other moons and Saturn's rings. The radar echoes will reveal the topography and composition of objects too small, or too smoggy, to be observed directly.

Cassini's other half, the Huygens probe, will take several hours to make a para-chute descent through Titan's atmosphere, and will then achieve a soft landing on the surface, where it should remain fully functional for at least half an hour. The probe will carry imagers and spectrometers to view the situation near and on Titan's surface and to determine the environment's composition. Huygens also carries an instru-ment that will trap aerosol particles, heat them, and determine the volatile com-pounds they contain. An acoustic sensor, activated during the final portion of the descent, will determine whether Titan's surface is solid or liquid and will measure properties such as the density, temperature, heat conductivity, heat capacity, and electrical conductivity of Titan's lower atmosphere.

At 12,346 pounds, the Cassini-Huygens spacecraft is the heaviest object that the United States has ever launched to distances far from Earth; the only heavier such craft were two Soviet probes sent to Mars, which never functioned properly. The Cassini orbiter weighs 4,750 pounds and the Huygens probe 770, while about 7,000 pounds of propellant will allow the spacecraft to maneuver through the Saturnian sys-tem for three or four years.

The most controversial aspect of the Cassini probe arises from its use of radioac-tive plutonium to generate the electricity that the spacecraft requires. At 9.5 times

Earth's distance from the sun, solar-power cells are impractical, and thermal radioisotopes such as plutonium, which release heat as they decay, can make the spacecraft run. Nevertheless, since plutonium is both extremely chemically toxic and quite highly radioactive, concern arose before Cassini's launch that an accident might spread these few lethal pounds of material over southern Florida, despite the best engineering efforts to keep the plutonium confined in case of an explosion. Although the Cassini spacecraft has been on its mission since October 1997, it still has a close pass to make by Earth in August 1999, which will give the spacecraft enough velocity from the gravitational-slingshot effect to send it on past Jupiter to Saturn. It remains possible, though not at all likely, that a miscalculation could cause Cassini to collide with Earth. NASA has judged these risks minimal, and so far has proven justified (for example, the Galileo spacecraft carried a similar radioisotope power supply and made a succcessful gravity-slingshot pass by Earth). The current of opinion, however, seems to be running against further use of plutonium to generate power for spacecraft missions, no matter how significant they may be.

For visits to the planets beyond Saturn, no spacecraft missions are now under construction. Our knowledge of these outer objects of the solar system comes largely from the plutonium-powered spacecraft Voyager 2, which passed by the sun's outermost large planets at the end of the 1980s. Let us revisit these successful encounters to see what Uranus and Neptune have to say for themselves.

URANUS AND NEPTUNE

Far beyond the sun's two largest planets, Jupiter and Saturn, lie the third- and fourth-largest, Uranus and Neptune. With masses between 15 and 20 times the Earth's mass and diameters about four times Earth's, Uranus and Neptune are near-twins of the solar system, matched as closely as Venus and Earth in size and mass. More than coincidence may lie behind the fact that twice in the solar system we find two similarly sized objects in successive planetary orbits, though astronomers' attempts to understand how the solar system formed cannot yet find such an explanation.

A journey to Uranus and Neptune carries us to distances from the sun much greater than Jupiter's or Saturn's. Uranus orbits the sun at 19.2 times the Earth-sun distance, more than twice as far as Saturn, and takes 84 years to complete each orbit, while Neptune, moving at 30 times our planet's distance from the sun, circles the sun every 165 years. Out by Uranus and Neptune, the sun fades to a small, pale version of the burning disk we know so well. Declining in proportion to the square of the observer's distance, the sun's apparent brightness falls to only $1/400$ at Uranus and to $1/900$ at Neptune of the brightness we observe on Earth. Uranus and Neptune capture only a tiny fraction of the sun's total energy output, and have correspondingly low temperatures, between minus 330 and minus 360 degrees Fahrenheit.

Less Gas, More Rock and Ice

Observations made from Earth-based telescopes and by the Voyager 2 spacecraft that passed by Uranus in 1986 and Neptune in 1989 show that these planets' outer layers consist of gases that include hydrogen, helium, and the simple molecules that hydrogen forms with carbon, nitrogen, hydrogen, sodium, and sulfur atoms. In particular, the two planets' atmospheres are rich in methane (CH4) and ammonia (NH3), which also exist in great amounts in the outer layers of Jupiter and Saturn. But unlike Jupiter and Saturn, the gaseous components of Uranus and Neptune do not dominate the planets' composition. Although their outer layers consist mainly of hydrogen and helium gas, the bulk of their interiors is a mixture of rock and ice. Astronomers have deduced this fact from their determinations of the planets' masses and sizes, coupled with calculations of how an object with 15 to 20 Earth masses will squeeze itself by self-gravitation. The rock-and-ice cores of Uranus and Neptune probably reach three-fourths of the way outward from the planets' centers, leaving the outermost one-quarter for the gas.

These large cores have changed little since the planets formed, 4.5 billion years ago. In particular, Uranus and Neptune, unlike Jupiter and Saturn, have essentially no internal sources of heat, because they lack the liquid hydrogen-and-helium interior

of Jupiter or the helium rain that keeps Saturn (relatively) warm. At the risk of disrespecting these two planets, we may say that not much happens inside them, and not much more outside. And (just to complain a bit more) they don't really look like much—certainly not in comparison with Jupiter and Saturn.

Why don't Uranus and Neptune look more interesting? All four of the sun's giant planets share the same basic composition of their gaseous outer layers, but the small admixtures of molecules that provides their colors must be quite different. Jupiter has a fine range of orange, brown, black, yellow, and red tints, whereas Saturn shows a much more delicate palette, centered on lemon-icing tones. Uranus, arguably the most boring of the planets, reveals coloration only when computers do their damnedest to exaggerate it. Neptune, in contrast to the

Uranus has a nearly featureless atmosphere, made up primarily of hydrogen, helium, methane, and ammonia.

other three, has rather lovely shades of blue, which arise because the planet's atmos-phere scatters sunlight much as the Earth's atmosphere does. Our finest spacecraft have not yet told us just which molecular compounds produce these colors, and laboratory experiments attempting to reproduce these shades have provided only inconclusive results. What is clear is that a small amount of color-giving com--pounds goes a long way, since the four most common constituents of the giant planets' atmospheres—hydrogen, helium, methane, and ethane—provide absolutely no color at all!

Planetary Rings

Like Jupiter and Saturn, Uranus and Neptune have rings of debris in orbit close to the planet. Uranus possesses thin, dark rings, first discovered as the planet passed between Earth and a distant star. Astronomers then saw repeated dips and rises in the amount of starlight reaching the Earth, which allowed them to deduce the rings' existence. Neptune has a similar ring system, likewise first noted by the planet's occultation of a faraway star. In Neptune's case, however, the material forming the rings has an uneven distribution around the orbits that mark a particular ring. This debris bunches up at certain points along the orbit like links in a string of sausage, apparently as the result of the interplay of gravitational forces exerted on the material by Neptune and its large moon, Triton.

The Tilt of Uranus

Uranus does have one claim to fame: the orientation of its rotation axis. Like other planets, Uranus rotates, and like the other giant planets, it rotates quickly, in just under 17 hours (Neptune rotates once every 16 hours). But unlike every other planet, Uranus's axis of rotation is not nearly perpendicular, or even approximately perpendicular, to the plane of the planet's orbit around the sun. Instead, Uranus's rotation axis lies nearly in that plane. Instead of being tilted by a familiar angle, such as the Earth's 23 $\frac{1}{2}$ degrees, from being perpendicular to its orbital plane, the axis around which Uranus rotates tilts by 82 degrees, close to the 90-degree value that would leave the rotation axis exactly in the planet's orbital plane. Since Jupiter, Saturn, and Neptune each tilt their rotation axes by less than 29 degrees (Jupiter by only 3 degrees, Saturn and Neptune by Earth-like values of 26.8 and 28.8 degrees, respectively), Uranus clearly ranks as an exception among the sun's planets. In fact, astronomers describe the tilt of Uranus's rotation axis not as 82 but as 98 degrees, meaning that the planet has tilted over by even more than a right angle, and now rotates in the opposite sense to the direction of its orbit around the sun.

Broadly speaking, Uranus rotates nearly in the plane of its orbit. Since its axis of rotation always points toward the same direction in space (as is true for the Earth and the other planets), this means that during its 84-year trip around the sun Uranus's northern hemisphere points almost toward the sun for 42 years, leaving the southern hemisphere in darkness, and then, after a slow interchange of day and night, the southern hemisphere undergoes its own 42-year-long sunlit spell, while the northern hemisphere goes through a lifelong winter. If Uranus had a solid surface, that entire surface would experience polar seasons so pronounced that Arctic and Antarctic summers and winters would seem by comparison momentary light and dark spells.

Uranus's unusual tilt in its rotation axis probably arose from a large impact soon after the time that Uranus formed. The "probably" here reflects the fact that impacts must have been likely—after all, smaller impacts built all the planets through agglomeration—and astronomers have no other good hypothesis to explain Uranus's exceptional rotation. Uranus has a bipolar magnetic field, similar in its contours to the Earth's, but unlike our planet, where the magnetic axis is roughly aligned with the rotation axis (which allows us to use a magnetic compass to estimate a northerly direction), Uranus's magnetic field is out of alignment, by about 60 degrees, from its rotation axis. This discrepancy surely must have arisen from the impact that originally tilted Uranus. But Neptune, with a "normal" tilt to its rotation axis, turns out to have a misalignment of its magnetic field that is nearly as large! On Neptune, the magnetic axis deviates by 55 degrees from its rotation axis. Scientists clearly have a long way to go in explaining how planets acquire their magnetic fields, how and why those fields align or misalign with the planets' rotation axes, and how and why the magnetic fields change in orientation and strength as the planets age.

Uranus's Satellites

Uranus has five medium-size moons, each the size of a modest country such as Belgium or Holland, and named after characters in Shakespeare's plays and Alexander Pope's poem *The Rape of the Lock*. After the Voyager 2 spacecraft discovered 10 more moons during its close passage by the planet in 1986, astronomers reached deeper into Shakespeare for 10 new names. All 15 of Uranus's moons move in nearly circular orbits above the planet's equator; hence their orbital planes, like Uranus's rotation axis, are tilted by nearly 90 degrees to the plane of the planet's orbit around the sun. The concept of exaggerated summers and winters, each 42 years long, therefore holds true for the moons, as the sun shines successively on each of their northern and southern hemispheres.

Uranus's five good-size moons, Miranda, Ariel, Umbriel, Titania, and Oberon, have diameters that range from 14 to 46 percent of our moon's diameter and orbital periods between 1.4 and 13.5 days. Like Saturn's satellites, Uranus's larger moons have densities that imply a composition mainly of ice, with some admixture of silicate rocks and metals; because the densities of Uranus's are somewhat higher than those of Saturn's moons, Uranus's satellites must include a lower proportion of ice. On Ariel and Umbriel, the second and third moons outward of the big five, Voyager photographed geological structures that include craters and long valleys, with some evidence for flow patterns; on Titania and Oberon, Voyager's images show heavily cratered surfaces.

By far the oddest of the big five moons is Miranda, the innermost and smallest of them, where Voyager's close encounter revealed a surface that has undergone enormous changes, the result of forces within the moon that remain basically mysterious to us. Miranda has giant valleys, some as deep as five or six miles, and the tallest sharp cliff in the solar system, nearly seven miles high; these must be the result of tectonic activity that testifies to internal changes within the satellite. This moon's surface also has strange, blocky mountain ranges, and a variety of craters, some with sharp, fresh-looking rims, others apparently eroded and softened. No one knows how a moon only 300 miles across could produce such a jagged and varied terrain. The satellite may have undergone sudden freezing soon after it formed, but this can hardly explain everything that Voyager saw. Future missions may someday land on Miranda to explore the reasons why it became such an oddity among the moons of the solar system.

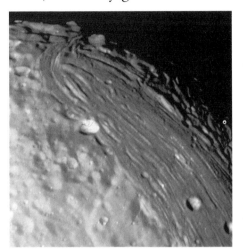

Uranus's moon Miranda displays a rich variety of geological features.

Neptune and Its Great Dark Spot

Neptune is much like Uranus, except for its color and its tilt, which are only modest variations on the basic theme of the smaller giant planets. In both Uranus and Neptune, a thick atmosphere envelops a core of rock and ice; wind currents produce muted, constantly changing patterns in that atmosphere; and the planets, far from the sun and with no internal source of heat, remain far colder than even Jupiter or Saturn.

In 1989, Voyager 2's flyby of Neptune showed not only that Neptune has a much more pronounced coloration than Uranus, but also that Neptune's atmosphere can

Neptune showed the Voyager 2 spacecraft its "Great Dark Spot," a cyclonic system that lasted for only a few years.

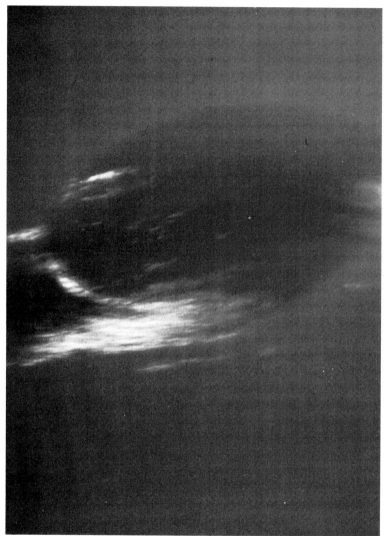

produce giant storm features. Voyager observed a "Great Dark Spot," which must have been a transitory cyclonic whorl, akin to Jupiter's Great Red Spot. At the edge of this Great Dark Spot, Voyager observed that white clouds would form and then dissipate within a few minutes. A few years after Voyager's visit, the Great Dark Spot had vanished; photographs taken by the Hubble Space Telescope during the mid-1990s showed a cool, blue, unspotted Neptune.

Triton and the Modest Moons

Neptune has one large satellite, named Triton (pronounced TRY-t'n) after one of the Roman sea god's children. About four-fifths the diameter of our own moon,

Triton had long drawn astronomers' attention for its unusual orbit, in which Triton moves around Neptune in the direction opposite to both Neptune's rotation and the direction in which Neptune and Triton orbit the sun. Triton's rotation is "locked" to its orbital period of 5.9 days, so that Triton always keeps the same side facing Neptune. However, Triton moves in a retrograde orbit, that is, in the direction opposite to the direction in which Neptune rotates and orbits the sun. This signals that Triton did not assemble itself from debris orbiting Neptune, all of which would have been orbiting in the same direction that Neptune rotates. Instead, Neptune's gravity must have captured Triton from a distance much greater than its current 220,000 miles, about 90 percent of the distance from the Earth to the moon. Since Triton closely resembles Pluto, which indeed it exceeds in size (Triton's diameter of 1,670 miles is less than our moon's 2,150 miles, but significantly greater than Pluto's 1,420 miles), we may easily conclude—at least until further evidence may cause us to reverse our opinion—that Triton once had an orbit of its own, similar to Pluto's, around the sun.

In addition to Triton, Neptune has seven much smaller satellites, six of which were discovered by Voyager 2 when it sailed past the Neptunian system. The one small satellite known to astronomers before Voyager, Nereid (pronounced NERR-ee-ed), has a diameter of just over 200 miles, and draws attention to itself by moving along the most highly elongated orbit of any planetary satellite. At its closest approach to Neptune, Nereid approaches Neptune to within about a million miles (still four times the moon's distance from the Earth), while at its farthest, Nereid reaches a distance seven times greater! It is easy to speculate that whatever process brought Triton in from a much greater distance to its present orbit, far inside Nereid's, must have perturbed Nereid through close encounters with the much larger and more massive new satellite of Neptune. These perturbations nearly ejected Nereid from the Neptunian system, but Neptune managed to retain Nereid in its present, highly elliptical orbit.

Triton has a density somewhat higher than those of the larger moons of Uranus, which implies a composition for the satellite of ice mixed with rock, much like the mixture in Titan and Jupiter's outer Galilean satellites, Ganymede and Callisto. Triton has one of the most highly reflective surfaces in the solar system, so it retains even less of the modest solar heat than we might expect, reflecting most of the incoming energy into space. This gives Triton the coldest surface temperature ever measured in the solar system, 410 degrees below zero Fahrenheit.

Neptune's large moon Triton has a thin atmosphere, replenished by geysers that erupt from its frozen surface.

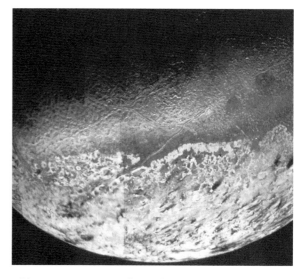

In 1989, Voyager 2 obtained fine photographs of Triton, which unexpectedly turned out to represent another unique character in the solar system. Triton has a thin atmosphere, made mainly of nitrogen, with some methane molecules. An unexpected source adds to and replenishes this atmosphere: geysers that blow plumes of gas from Triton's surface! At minus 410 Fahrenheit, geysers hardly seem likely, but they do exist. Triton must have some modest sources of heat near its surface that release material in sudden spurts, rising as much as five miles high.

With Triton we have met the first of the smaller objects in the outer reaches of the solar system—objects that all resemble comets in their composition, and perhaps in their origin as well. Pluto and its satellite Charon fit this description; so too do the "trans-Plutonian" objects, not planets but not exactly comets, that astronomers have recently discovered. Let us sail farther from the sun to explore the objects that no spacecraft has visited, but which maintain, locked within their pristine iciness, the secrets of how the solar system formed.

CHAPTER ELEVEN

THE OUTER SOLAR SYSTEM

Judging by the mass of objects, the sun, its eight planets (not counting Pluto), and their large satellites fill out the basic census of the solar system, which can omit the planets' smaller moons, as well as all the asteroids and meteoroids, without missing much in the mass game. If we insist on describing objects with relatively low masses, we ought to record that out beyond Neptune, orbiting the sun at distances from 40 to thousands of times the Earth-sun distance, are a host of objects. Most of these are comets, but a few are icy objects, somewhat similar to comets but distinguished from the true comets by their sizes and their orbits. By far the largest of these icy trans-Neptunian objects is Pluto, and firmly in second place in size and mass is Pluto's satellite, Charon. We may pay Pluto and Charon the courtesy of a detailed look before we survey the smaller, Pluto-like objects that astronomers have recently discovered at still greater distances from the sun.

The Discovery of Pluto

Pluto was discovered in 1930 by Clyde Tombaugh, a young assistant at the Lowell Observatory in Arizona, who had been assigned the task of scrutinizing photographic plates as part of an organized search to find a planet beyond Neptune. Just as astronomers had deduced Neptune's existence from Uranus's deviations from its predicted position, so too careful analysis of the observations of Neptune's changing position revealed a divergence from the positions predicted in the absence of any trans-Neptunian planet. Calculations that relied on astronomers' understanding of the gravitational forces among the planets and the sun implied that a planet with a mass comparable to Neptune's should be orbiting the sun at a distance significantly greater than Neptune's; the calculations also indicated the region of the sky where "Planet X" could be found.

Although Percival Lowell had created the Lowell Observatory primarily to study the planet Mars, about a decade after Lowell's death in 1916 the observatory shifted its focus and began to survey the region of the sky where a trans-Neptunian planet might be found. The search proceeded by taking two or more long-exposure photographs of each part of the sky to be surveyed. Astronomers then used a specialized apparatus to hold a pair of photographic plates taken several weeks or months apart. This machine carefully aligned two plates showing the identical set of stars at the same scale of magnification. The apparatus had a mirror that could "blink" back and forth between the two plates, revealing first one plate and then the other. As the observer blinked a pair of plates, any object that had moved in orbit during the time between the two exposures would seem to jump back and forth against the background of stationary stars.

Using this method, Tombaugh and others at the observatory found many jumping objects, most of them previously undetected asteroids and comets at distances from the sun roughly comparable to Jupiter's. These objects jumped by much greater amounts than would an object moving much more slowly in orbit, at a distance closer to 10 times Jupiter's. Finally, however, Tombaugh found a trans-Neptunian object, moving at just about the speed anticipated for Planet X. Additional observations confirmed this object's orbit, and in March 1930, on Lowell's 75th birthday, the observatory announced the new addition to the solar system. Pluto's astronomical symbol became an entwined *P* and *L*, incorporating Lowell's initials in honor of his pioneering efforts in solar-system observations. Struggling amid a worldwide depression, the public found the new planet a cheery reminder that our troubles are transitory, the planets long-lived. The fact that Pluto has a rather tenuous claim to true planethood lay gently in wait, ready to provide future discussions among astronomical cognoscenti.

Pluto has the most elongated of all the planets' orbits, a 248-year-long elliptical trajectory that carries it from its average distance from the sun of 39 times the Earth-sun distance as far outward as 49.3 times that distance and as far inward as 29.6 times. Since Neptune moves in a nearly circular orbit at 30.1 times the Earth-sun distance, this means that at its points of closest approach (for example, during the final years of the twentieth century), Pluto comes inside Neptune's orbit. We might anticipate a collision between the two, but this can never occur: Neptune and Pluto are in a "3-to-2 resonance," with Neptune making three trips around the sun (taking 164.8 years for each one) for every two by Pluto. Whenever Pluto reaches perihelion (the point of closest approach to the sun), Neptune is on the opposite side, far across the solar system. Nevertheless, the fact that Pluto's perihelion distance almost exactly equals Neptune's orbital distance suggests that interactions between Pluto and the Neptune-Triton system may indeed have occurred in the far distant past, and that the 3-to-2 resonance came slowly into play, long after these interactions.

Does Pluto Qualify as a Planet?

Pluto's discovery seemed at first to be another triumph of celestial mechanics, a tribute to astronomers' computational and observational abilities. Only one problem appeared to spoil this perfection: Pluto shone far less than anyone expected for a planet with a size comparable to Neptune's. A good pair of binoculars will easily show Neptune, and would also reveal a Neptune-like planet at a distance only one-third greater. In fact, however, Pluto has an apparent brightness only about $1/100$ of Neptune's. This low brightness implies a small size and correspondingly small mass. Today, although Pluto remains unvisited by any spacecraft, photographs from the Hubble Space Telescope, and measurements by ground-based instruments, show that Pluto has a diameter 70 percent of our moon's and a mass only 16 percent of the moon's. This object cannot possibly produce any perturbations in Neptune's orbit of the size that led to Pluto's discovery. In fact, subsequent reanalyses of Neptune's motion have shown that the original "perturbations" were apparently spurious. Hence Pluto's discovery had an utterly incorrect motivation—yet there it is!

What is it? This question has no easy answer. An object smaller than our moon, with an average density half of the moon's, must be made primarily of ice, and has only a tenuous claim to rank as a planet. In addition to our own satellite, six of the giant planets' moons have more mass than Pluto; three of them, Ganymede, Titan, and Triton, have roughly 10 times more. On the other hand, Pluto is nobody's satellite but the sun's. On the third hand, the same can be said of the asteroids, meteoroids, and comets, which no one calls planets.

Finally, Pluto has a satellite of its own, and not a small one either. Pluto's moon, named Charon (pronounced KARE-on) after the ferryman of the dead (for Pluto was lord of the underworld), has almost half of Pluto's diameter and one-tenth its mass.

Pluto, by far the smallest object that we might call a planet, has a satellite, Charon, with nearly half Pluto's diameter.

Even though we now know that at least some asteroids have satellites of their own, the possession of a moon 600 miles in diameter strengthens Pluto's claim to planetary ranking. Furthermore, even though Pluto's composition,

like that of Charon and of Neptune's large moon Triton, does resemble that of a comet, the largest known comets have diameters of 50 to 100 miles, not the 1,400 miles that characterize Pluto. The notable difference in size between even the largest comets on the one hand, and Pluto, Charon, and Triton on the other, implies that we should pause before announcing that these three objects are simply giant comets. Most astronomers would argue that the true discriminant between planets and comets lies in the objects' histories. As we saw in Chapter 3, the planets formed after the rotating disk of gas and dust surrounding the protosun had contracted to roughly the present size of the planets' orbits. In contrast, most of the comets formed at earlier times, when the disk was still shrinking; many of these comets then built the planets by agglomeration. If we could tell whether Pluto formed much farther from the sun that it is now, we could decide whether to name it a planet or a comet. For now, in view of the effort that millions have devoted to learning the nine planets in orbit, this book will tilt toward planetary status. On the other hand . . .

Since Pluto's icy composition resembles that of a comet, we can hardly be surprised that Pluto on occasion behaves like a comet. When Pluto reaches the point on its orbit closest to the sun, it receives an amount of solar energy 80 percent greater than it does at its average distance. At these times, the sun's heat evaporates some of the nitrogen that otherwise lies frozen on Pluto's surface. Pluto thus acquires a highly rarefied atmosphere of nitrogen molecules during each close approach to our star.

The Nature of Comets

We have now met planets and their satellites, along with asteroids and meteoroids, on our tour of the solar system. To complete the list of objects in orbit around the sun, we must turn to the solar system's oldest, least altered members, made of frozen material that remained behind after the planets and their moons had formed. These are the comets, the dirty snowballs that typically remain far from the sun, orbiting through the wasteland of interplanetary space.

In the history of modern understanding of comets and the role that they play in the solar system, three names stand out, two Dutch and one American. The American, Fred Whipple, produced the basic model to describe the composition of a comet. The two Dutch astronomers, Gerard Kuiper and Jan Oort, studied cometary motions and drew sweeping conclusions about the orbits that the comets follow. As we saw in Chapter 3, these orbits reveal how comets have interacted with the larger objects in the solar system.

Comets represent primordial parts of the solar system, pieces that long ago built the planets and their satellites. Astronomers draw this conclusion from their hypotheses of how the solar system formed, from a contracting, rotating pancake of matter that once was part of a much larger interstellar cloud of gas and dust. Within this pancake, subclumps grew by agglomeration to become the planets and their large satellites, while smaller bits of matter, of much the same sort that had gone into the larger objects, continued to orbit the sun as meteoroids, asteroids, and the small satellites of Mars and the giant planets.

Assuming this hypothesis to be true, we may ask: Can we identify remnants of the original rotating pancake in addition to the objects we have listed above? The answer seems clear: Those remnants are the comets, most of which orbit the sun in highly elongated trajectories that keep them at distances thousands of times the Earth's distance from the sun. Each comet, Fred Whipple proposed more than four decades ago, is a dirty snowball, a mixture of ordinary ice, solid carbon dioxide ("dry ice"), and solid carbon monoxide, which has frozen around an assortment of pebbles, rocks, boulders, and even larger solid objects. Typical comets are five or ten miles across, and have masses comparable to the mass of a mountain on Earth.

So hypothesized Whipple on the basis of observations and theory. All of our comet observations, however, deal with a comet not in its usual state but rather as we see the comet, when it approaches the sun to within Jupiter's distance or less. To detect, let alone to study, an object only a few miles across at distances much beyond Jupiter's lies beyond even the finest telescopes, partly because comets' dirty snow reflects sunlight only poorly, and even more because we are attempting to observe astronomically tiny objects. Only a few comets, such as Halley's, which have well-calculated orbits and a strong call on telescope time, have received the special attention that can reveal them to our view at distances as great as those of Saturn or Uranus.

When Halley's Comet came close to the sun in 1986, Japanese and European spacecraft flew past it, taking pictures that vindicated Whipple's dirty-snowball model. Like all the comets that pass inside Jupiter's orbit, Halley's underwent a visually striking transformation, one that will eventually lead to the comet's destruction. Solar heating warmed the comet's outer layers, vaporizing its outermost few inches or feet. This warmed-over matter formed a fuzzy coma around the basic

comet, which astronomers call the cometary nucleus, and some of the material from the coma was pushed away from the sun to create the famous tail of a comet, millions of miles long but made of such undense material that if the tail were compressed to the density of water, it would fit easily into an ordinary suitcase.

A comet's tail always points away from the sun as the result of two types of interactions. Sunlight pushes on the dust particles, creating one or more dust tails, while the fast-moving particles (mostly protons and electrons) expelled from the sun in the "solar wind" push on the much smaller atoms and molecules, creating a gas tail. The comet's coma and tail evaporate into the regions surrounding the comet, diminishing it by the amount of lost material. Every close pass by the sun therefore reduces the comet a bit, until, as astronomers have observed in several instances, the comet breaks apart into small pieces that no longer deserve the title of comet.

Halley's Comet exhibits typical behavior each time that it passes close to the sun, but its orbit ranks as nearly unique among all comets. Several thousand of these are short-period comets, which have been captured by the gravitational effects of the sun's most massive planet, and move around the sun along notably elongated orbits whose periods resemble those of Jupiter, typically between 5 and 18 years. The best-known short-term comet, because its relatively small orbit carries it close to the

When a comet comes near the sun, solar heating produces a fuzzy "coma" and a long, gauzy tail, made of gas and dust that always points away from the sun.

The orbit of Halley's Comet carries it inside the orbit of Venus and outside the orbit of Neptune.

Earth, is Encke's Comet, whose 3.3-year trajectory carries it inside Mercury's orbit and well outside the orbit of Mars. Halley's Comet, which takes 76 years for each orbit, passes out beyond Neptune and then inside Venus's orbit on each trip around the sun; it might be called a medium-period comet if we could find other comets with orbits that take about a century to complete.

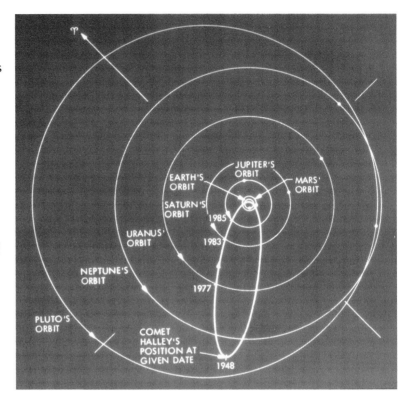

The Oort Cloud

The vast majority of comets are long-period comets, numbering in the hundreds of billions, or perhaps even a trillion or so. Always remaining at hundreds or thousands of times the Earth's distance from the sun, these comets take thousands of years, or even tens or hundreds of thousands of years, to make a single trip around the sun. The most famous of these comets is… In actuality, astronomers have yet to see, let alone identify, a single long-period comet in one of the giant orbits described above. Instead, following Jan Oort's original calculations, they deduce that these billions or trillions of comets must exist from the fact that some of them are continually diverted into orbits that bring them relatively close to the sun. Gravitational effects from Jupiter and Saturn can then change the comets' orbits still further, so that they become short-period comets, or—on some verified occasions—a comet will head back outward into the depths of interstellar space.

Oort proposed that if we seek to explain even the small number of new comets that enter the inner solar system in a human lifetime, we must imagine a mighty reservoir of comets, which astronomers now call the Oort cloud. (Oort himself, one of the gentlest and most determined of astronomers, would never have suggested such a name.) A small flaw in the Oort cloud reservoir model arises from the fact that we really don't know what processes divert comets from their usual orbits. Gravitational interactions, either among comets or between comets and stars that slowly pass by at immense distances, seem the likely explanation, but a good theory of just how this occurs remains to be found. This gap in our understanding affects the extrapolation by which astronomers deduce the total number of comets in the Oort cloud from the few that we see when they approach the sun. Let us, without much danger of criticism, round off to one trillion comets in the Oort cloud, a mighty number worthy of the man himself.

Does this mean that comets form the dominant component of the solar system? Not if we reckon by mass rather than by numbers. A typical comet, with a nucleus only a few miles across, has a mass about one ten-billionth of the Earth's. Hence even a trillion comets have a total mass roughly 100 times the Earth's, or one-third of Jupiter's mass. And there may not be as many as a trillion comets; a few tens or hundreds of billions may suffice to explain all that we see.

Since the Oort cloud consists of a trillion comets or so, all at immense distances from the sun, we might be tempted to conclude that these comets, which collectively occupy about the same volume as the original subclump of an interstellar cloud that became the solar system, are in fact the remnants of that clump. This conclusion, though correct in one aspect, misses the mark in another. The comets in the Oort cloud are indeed the oldest pieces of the solar system, which formed shortly before the sun began to shine, more than 4.5 billion years ago. But the Oort cloud comets have their huge orbits not because they were born out there but because they were flung out there. All the comets in the Oort cloud once belonged to the Kuiper belt.

The Kuiper Belt

The basic scenario describing the formation of the solar system that we described in Chapter 3 envisions a subclump of an interstellar cloud, originally as large as the current Oort cloud, that contracted and flattened over millions of years, producing a rotating pancake of matter with a diameter many dozens or hundreds or even thousands of times larger than the Earth's orbit around the sun. Within that pancake, smaller clumps assembled themselves as cometlike objects collided and stuck together. Some of these clumps eventually attracted enough matter to become the four inner and the four giant planets, along with their major satellites.

This process left a host of the cometlike objects in orbit around the sun, part of the pancake of matter that had been transforming itself into individual good-size objects. Any comet that happened to pass close to Jupiter or Saturn (and, to a lesser extent, close to Uranus and Neptune or even to Venus and the Earth) would have undergone one of two fates. Either the comet would have been incorporated into the newly formed planets, or—more often than intuition would suggest—the encounter would have flung the comet into a much larger orbit, far out into the Oort cloud.

The objects that joined neither the planets nor the Oort cloud remained as the Kuiper belt, the fossil remnants of the rotating disk of matter that made the entire solar system 4.5 billion years ago. Out beyond the orbit of Pluto, moving forever through the frigid transition zone where interplanetary space merges into the interstellar medium, the objects in the Kuiper belt guard their pristine secrets, barely altered during more than 4 billion years. For decades, astronomers believed in the existence of the Kuiper belt, but they knew next to nothing about KBOs, the Kuiper belt objects (unless we denote as KBOs the icy objects Triton, Pluto, and Charon, which almost certainly once formed part of the Kuiper belt and were captured from it into smaller orbits). Finally, in 1992, Jane Luu and David Jewett made the first definitive observations of a KBO, designated as 1992QB$_I$, which has an average distance from the sun about 20 percent greater than Pluto's and takes 296 years to complete an orbit around the sun. With this discovery, the KBO floodgates metaphorically opened, and astronomers proceeded to find more than three dozen similar objects, all of which have diameters of about 50 miles and orbits much like that of 1992QB$_I$. Improved techniques have now begun to reveal still smaller objects, moving in similar trajectories around the sun. The Kuiper belt has proven to be real; all that remains is to make the next step in studying it by sending spacecraft to 40 or 50 times the Earth-sun distance to sample these frozen relics.

Far from the sun though the KBOs may be, a trip to the Kuiper belt will hardly take us to the closest stars. For that, we must travel roughly a thousand times farther—a ratio that must never be forgotten when someone tries to convince you that extraterrestrials from other planetary systems have taken the long trip to Earth. Despite this enormous ratio, and despite the fact that planets around other stars must be lost to visibility in their parents' glaring light, astronomers have recently managed to discover planets around some of the sun's closer neighbors. This effort and success deserve a closer look, which foretells a new millennial era, during which our knowledge of planets around other stars will pass from a rudimentary to a robust condition.

CHAPTER TWELVE

WORLDS UNNUMBERED: FINDING PLANETS AROUND OTHER STARS

Astronomers have long recognized that our sun qualifies as a representative star, a bit more luminous than the average but nevertheless a prime-of-life, nuclear-fusing ball of gas much like most of the other stars that sparkle in the night skies. This naturally raises the question: Does the sun's retinue of planets, along with the host of lesser objects that orbit the sun, furnish a good example of what surrounds the average star?

For decades on end, astronomers have had to answer this question with the pious hope that at some future time, we shall be able to observe planets around other stars, and thus to determine the accuracy with which our solar system models the typical surroundings of a star. Astronomers could cite only this hope, with no actual sightings of planets around other stars, for the excellent reason that we cannot observe any planets that may orbit stars beyond the sun.

This negative statement refers to any attempt to see a planet with a conventional, Earth-bound telescope and arises from a combination of two factors: Stars are extremely distant and luminous; in contrast, any planets that may orbit these stars, by definition as well as in actual fact, are just as distant, emit no visible light of their own, and shine only dimly by the starlight they reflect. Thus any "extrasolar planets" must remain lost in the glare of their nearby parent stars, hidden from our view because no telescope can reveal a faint point of light so close to a bright star.

To drive this point home, consider a distant civilization, living on a planet orbiting another star, that hopes to observe planets around our sun. Earth, the largest inner planet, intercepts one part in a billion of the sun's total output, reflecting about half of the light that strikes it while absorbing the remainder. Jupiter, 11 times larger than Earth but orbiting at 5.2 times Earth's distance, intercepts about 40 percent as much solar energy as the Earth does, and also reflects about half of the solar energy that falls on it. Thus any distant observer searching for planets around our sun would have to discover objects that shine with less than one-billionth of the sun's apparent brightness.

By itself, this brightness ratio would offer no insuperable obstacle. Astronomers routinely observe objects whose apparent brightness equals not one-billionth but a mere one hundred-billionth of the apparent brightness of the stars close to the sun. What renders impossible the discovery of extrasolar planets by conventional methods is the combination of the planets' low apparent brightness with their proximity to their stars. The distance from the sun to Alpha Centauri, the closest star system, equals 4.4 light years, approximately 280,000 times the distance from the Earth to the sun, and more than 50,000 times the distance between Jupiter and the sun. Nearby stars such as Sirius (8 light years from the solar system) and Vega (26 light years away) are roughly one million times farther from Earth than the sun.

To observe planets around nearby stars, astronomers must "resolve"—see as separate points of light—two objects whose angular separation in the sky is measured in seconds of arc. One second of arc, the angular size of a dime seen from a distance of three miles, equals the angular separation between the sun and Jupiter, when observed from a distance of 16 light years. Astronomers often observe double- and triple-star systems in which the individual stars have angular separations comparable to this, but success in their efforts depends on the fact that the stars have roughly equal brightnesses. They cannot hope to resolve two objects separated by one second of arc if one of the objects shines a billion times more brightly than the other. Instead, they must use indirect methods in their attempts to determine whether planets exist around other stars. The most fruitful of these techniques has also been the least direct: observations not of planets but of the stuff from which planets are made.

Planetary Disks Around Other Stars

Planets lock most of their matter inside them, making it useless for reflecting light. In contrast, the early stages of planet formation, when objects slowly grow by gathering material within a disk of gas and dust, allow a much greater fraction of the existing material to reflect light or to emit infrared and radio waves. For this reason, astronomers have detected "protoplanetary disks," the predecessors of actual planetary systems, more readily (though still not without great effort) than actual extrasolar planets. The recent discovery of protoplanetary disks around many nearby stars demonstrates that at least the initial stages of planet formation are a common occurrence.

Most of these discoveries have come from mapping the regions close to nearby stars in their emission of infrared radiation or short-wavelength radio waves, the types of radiation produced by warm dust. In hundreds of cases, astronomers have found disks of material, rotating around relatively young stars, that have the potential to generate planets some day. In a few of these instances, the disks show clearings at their centers, with diameters roughly equal to the solar system's diameter out to the orbit of Pluto. Such a clearing is just what the standard model of planet formation predicts. As planets grow larger, their gravitational forces will attract nearly all the nearby dust and gas, leaving their immediate surroundings free of this debris, while the disk outside the planet-forming region, that system's Kuiper belt (no doubt differently named out there), remains largely unchanged.

The most persuasive example of a disk with a clearing appears around a star called HR4796, about 220 light years from Earth in the direction of the constellation Centaurus. In April 1998, astronomers announced that they had used telescopes in Chile and Hawaii to map a disk of material around this star by the infrared radiation it emits. The disk spans a distance several times the diameter of the sun's planetary system and clearly has a hole at its center, a bit larger than the diameter of Pluto's orbit. Because astronomers can assign an age of 10 million years to HR4796 with some confidence, this star now represents the likeliest example of a young, nearby planetary system observed as it forms, or just afterward. Other disks with holes exist around stars such as Fomalhaut, one of the brightest stars in the sky, but the ages of these stars are much less certain.

We can easily imagine that new planets exist around HR4796, and that these planets are starting to experience a great era of bombardment, similar to what occurred in the solar system about 4.6 billion years ago. But we must call this imagination; for now, we have no proof that any planets have actually formed around this star. Until just a few years ago, that negative statement would have summed up the situation regarding planets around other stars. A dramatic reversal of fortune, however, has changed astronomers' dreams into realities, for they have now made definitive detections of extrasolar planets.

Seven Approaches to Finding Planets Around Other Stars

As the millennium draws to a close, astronomers have developed, or are working on, seven different methods to search for extrasolar planets rather than planetary disks. These techniques involve the use of astrometry, of Doppler shifts, of planetary transits, of gravitational microlensing, of interferometry, of pulsar timing, and of the search for extraterrestrial intelligence. Two of these, the Doppler-shift and pulsar-timing methods, have already met with success. The other five have yet to reveal any planets, though astrometry seems poised on the brink. While postponing discussion of the alien-intelligence method for the next chapter, we may take a look at the other six ways that astronomers can use to find planets orbiting other stars in the Milky Way.

Number One: Astrometry

Planets orbit their stars in response to a star's gravitational force. As it orbits, each planet exerts an equal amount of gravitational force on the star; however, as we saw in Chapter 2, the star accelerates far less than the planet does, because the star has far more mass than the planet. Nevertheless, the star does move, performing a tiny orbit that mimics that of the planet in shape and duration. In a system with several planets, the star's orbit becomes complex, but its movement still exists, and can, at least in theory, be observed. Astrometry, which means measurement of the stars, relies on making a series of observations of a star's position, which may reveal the effects produced by the gravitational forces of any planets that may orbit the star.

Complicating these observations is the fact that both the star and our solar system are moving in orbit around the center of the Milky Way galaxy, and that as the solar system moves in the Milky Way, we on Earth also orbit the sun. Attempts to observe the tiny motions of another star in response to its planets' gravity can therefore proceed only by dealing with three much greater motions. Astronomers must allow for the Earth's yearly motion in orbit around the sun, for the motion of the sun and its planets around the Milky Way, and for the other star's similar, though not identical, movement around our galaxy.

For the first planets discovered around sunlike stars, this diagram shows the planets' masses, in units of Jupiter's mass, and their distances from their parent stars, in units of the Earth-sun distance (1 astronomical unit, or A.U.). The diagram also shows Jupiter and Saturn, and notes the elongations of the planets' orbits (e = 0 denotes a circular orbit; e = 0.38, a markedly elongated one).

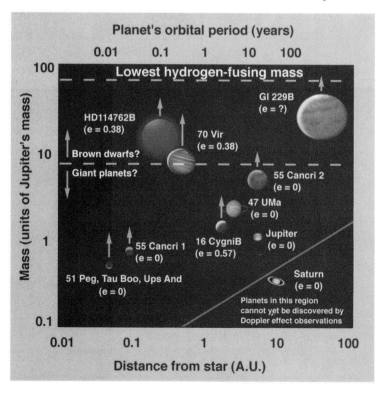

The first subtraction has a long lineage, because the Earth's motion produces stellar parallax shifts, back-and-forth changes in position that nearby stars perform against the backdrop of much more distant stars during the course of a year. The amount of a star's parallax shift varies in inverse proportion to the star's distance from us. This allows astronomers to determine the distances to nearby stars by measuring their parallax shifts. When astronomers record a series of measurements of a nearby star's position, they can take account of its parallax shift, removing its effects from the positions they plot for the star in the sky.

The next two motions can be dealt with as a single combination. The difference between the sun's motion and that of a nearby star around the galactic center gives rise to a star's "proper motion," its individual (the old meaning of the word proper) motion on the dome of heaven. If a star's orbit around the Milky Way exactly matched the sun's, it would have zero proper motion, but almost every star has an orbit whose speed and orientation differ slightly from the sun's. The more the star's orbit differs from our own, the greater will be its proper motion, after allowing for the fact that more distant stars will have their proper motions reduced because the same difference in speed will appear as a smaller distance in angular displacement.

Careful observations over many years will reveal the proper motion of nearby stars. If these stars have no planets, their proper motions should appear as straight lines across the background of more distant stars. (Since stars take hundreds of millions of years to orbit the Milky Way, "many years" on Earth reveal such a small portion of the complete orbit that a straight line provides an excellent fit to the star's trajectory.) If a nearby star has planets, however, its proper motion should show "wobbles," deviations first to one side and then to the other of its basic proper-motion path. The amount(s) of these wobbles can reveal the mass(es) of the planet(s) around another star, and the time(s) for a cycle of deviation can reveal the planets' orbital period(s).

Even a massive planet around one of the closest stars will produce only tiny deviations from straight-line proper motion, just at the limit of astronomers' abilities to measure. In recent years, astronomers have developed more accurate astrometric methods and a better understanding of their observational errors; they now stand on the brink of finding extrasolar planets with this technique, though they have not yet made definitive detections by astrometry. Those have come through an entirely different technique, based on the colors of starlight.

Doppler Shifts: The Path to Recent Success

During the past few years, the search for extrasolar planets has borne fine fruit: Astronomers have now identified more planets outside the solar system than exist inside it. Their success has come mainly from employing the Doppler effect to find planets. Like astrometry, this method involves observing stars to detect the effects of their planets. In this case, however, astronomers are searching for changes not in a star's position but in its velocity.

Familiar to all of us from our happy days in high-school physics, the Doppler effect describes the changes that we observe in the light from a star that is moving toward us or away from us. If the star moves toward us, its decreasing distance toward the observer makes successive crests of light waves reach us more often. This increases the frequencies (the number of vibrations per second) of the light waves we detect, while it decreases their wavelengths (the distances between successive wave crests). In contrast, the motion of a star away from us stretches the intervals between wave crests, so the frequency decreases and the wavelength increases. More rapid motion produces greater "Doppler shifts," the changes caused by the Doppler effect, which do not depend on whether the source of waves is moving, the observer is moving, or both are moving. To our eyes, the frequency and wavelength of light waves appear as colors; the longest wavelengths we can perceive appear red, the shortest violet. The Doppler effect would cause a driver approaching a red light at 80,000 miles per second (nearly half the speed of light) to see the light's color as green (not a serviceable excuse).

Measurement of the various features in a star's spectrum of light will sometimes reveal periodic, repetitive variations, which shift all the frequencies and wavelengths alternately toward the red and then toward the violet ends of the visible-light spectrum. Such cyclical changes allow astronomers to deduce the existence of a nearby object, whose gravitational force pulls the star alternately in opposite directions as the two objects orbit their common center of mass, changing the amount of the Doppler shift in a periodic fashion. Astronomers had long used this method to find companion stars in orbit with another star; recently, they have employed the technique to find far less massive planets around stars dozens of light years from the solar system.

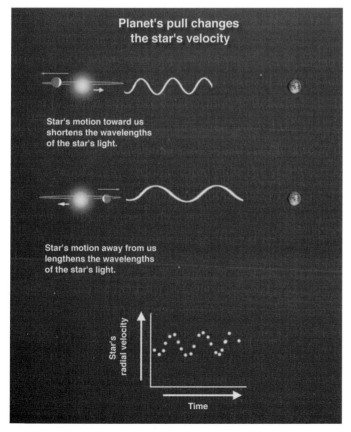

As we know, a star will accelerate in response to its planet's gravitational force, but by far less than the planet accelerates in response to the equal amount of gravitational force from the star. Planets in orbit around other stars move at speeds of many miles per second, but their stars move at speeds measured in yards per second. To find extrasolar planets by the Doppler effect, astronomers must therefore

The Doppler effect changes all the wavelengths, and therefore the colors, of the light from a distant star, by amounts that depend on the star's velocity toward or away from the Earth.

detect the Doppler shifts that arise from these modest speeds. If they can do so, and if they find that the Doppler shifts recur in a definite cycle, they may reasonably conclude that something tugs the star, first in one direction and then in the opposite direction. The time interval for the cycle to repeat itself reveals the orbital period of the object pulling the star, and further analysis will reveal the object's mass, and even the deviation from circularity of its orbit.

To reach an accuracy of a few yards per second in Doppler-shift measurements required several decades of hard work, which finally paid off in 1995 when the first extrasolar planet around a sunlike star was detected by the Doppler method. Three years later, astronomers had discovered more than a dozen planetlike objects in orbit around sunlike stars in our corner of the Milky Way. Some of these objects may turn out to be "brown dwarfs," objects with more than ten times the mass of Jupiter, generating large amounts of heat by their slow contraction; most of them, however, appear to be true planets, with masses that range from about half of Jupiter's mass to about five times Jupiter's.

These extrasolar planets have amazed astronomers, not by how they are but by where they are: Half of them orbit their sunlike stars at distances less than one-sixth of the distance from the sun to Mercury. This raises sizable problems in explaining how planets with Jupiter-like masses come to orbit so close to their parent stars.

Astronomers' current models of how planets form draw deeply on the example provided by our own solar system; they cannot explain the formation of planets with Jupiter-like masses so close to their parent stars as the recently discovered giant planets. Because a star's heat will evaporate the lightest, most abundant elements, all the models conclude that an object can accumulate a mass comparable to Jupiter's only if it forms at distances from a star at least three to four times greater than the Earth-sun distance. Hence, attempts to explain how planets with Jupiter-like masses have come to orbit their stars at distances about one $1/100$ of the Jupiter-sun distance require that these planets formed themselves a hundred times farther away from the star, and then somehow moved inward only after they had acquired their large masses. These explanations invoke gravitational interactions between the remnants of the disk that gave birth to the planets and the new-born planets themselves, with the disk tugging the planets inward as it evaporates.

If these models should prove correct, even in approximation, they lead to the

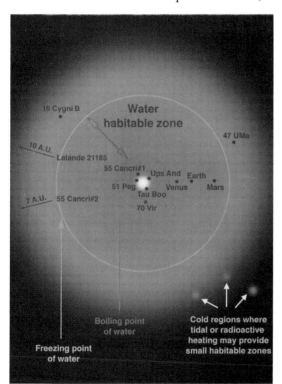

conclusion that any process that moves Jupiter-like planets inward toward their stars will almost surely consume planets that may have formed in orbits similar to the Earth's orbit around the sun. These might-have-been Earths would be caught by the gravitational forces from the larger planets, becoming part of the giant planets as they migrate inward toward their stars. Thus the recent discoveries, though they encourage those who search for other worlds, also imply that Earth-like planets may be rarer than we once thought, because the process described above seems to eliminate the possibility of Earth-like planets at Earth-like distances from their stars.

The habitable zone around a sunlike star specifies the region, neither too hot nor too cold, where water could exist as a liquid. Most of the recently discovered planets lie too close to their stars to fall within the stars' habitable zones.

Not all of the newly discovered objects move in the small orbits described above. One of them, around the star 70 Virginis, 72 light years from Earth, has an orbit 43 percent of the size of Earth's. On the other hand, of all the recently discovered objects, this one is the prime candidate for being a brown dwarf rather than a true planet, especially as its orbit is much more elongated than any planet's orbit in the solar system.

Because the amounts of the Doppler shifts increase as the planet-star distances decrease, the Doppler-effect method favors finding close-in objects. Hosts of farther-out planets presumably still await our detection. However, a key conclusion from the first planets discovered around sunlike stars seems to be that if we want to find Earth-like planets, we must do more than find Jupiter-like planets and deduce from them that smaller planets exist in the same planetary system. Instead, we must plan to discover those other Earths directly. This is a far more difficult task, which calls into play other techniques for finding extrasolar planets.

The Transit Method

Most stars shine steadily, varying in luminosity by less than one percent over the course of many years. Because of this constancy, an observer who carefully monitors the brightness of distant stars might see a sudden drop, if the geometry of the situation was such that a Jupiter-size planet happened to pass directly in front of the star. The "transit" of Jupiter across the sun would diminish the sun's apparent brightness by about one part in a hundred, since Jupiter has one-tenth of the sun's diameter, while a transit of Earth would cause a brightness decrease by one part in ten thousand.

These facts have led some astronomers to suggest launching a satellite designed to monitor the apparent brightnesses of hundreds or thousands of stars, waiting for the dip caused by a planetary transit. This modest diminution in brightness would last for a few hours or days, as the planet's motion carried it in front of the star. A transit-seeking satellite could avoid the distortions caused by the Earth's atmosphere, which tend to mask brightness changes below the one-percent level. Stars to be studied by the transit method need not be particularly close, since the changes in their brightnesses do not depend on the distance. To be sure that a transit had occurred, rather than an internal change in the star's brightness, we would have to wait for the next transit, which would also reveal the planet's orbital period. Hence the search for extrasolar planets by the transit method must be a multiyear undertaking, one that for the time being remains a proposal rather than a definitive undertaking.

Gravitational Microlensing

Albert Einstein's theory of general relativity, published in 1916, made a startling pronouncement: Gravity bends space. As a result of this bending, light rays will deviate from straight-line trajectories in passing close to a massive object such as a star. Einstein's theory received triumphant vindication at the total solar eclipse of May 29, 1919, when scientific expeditions photographed the stars visible near the edge of the moon-covered sun during totality. By comparing their new photographs with earlier ones, astronomers measured a bending of starlight in the same direction, and of the same amount, that Einstein's theory predicted.

Since gravitational forces bend light, we can imagine some alignments of objects in which the gravitational bending spreads light rays apart, and others in which the bending focuses the light rays, producing an increase in an object's apparent brightness. In some situations an impressive focusing can occur, increasing the object's apparent brightness by ten or a hundred times. Astrophysicists call these increases "gravitational microlensing." They can occur when astronomers observe a distant star at just the time when another, somewhat closer star happens to come between Earth and the distant star: The intervening star temporarily focuses and brightens the light from the farther star. If the intervening star has a planet in orbit around it, that planet's gravitational force can produce a similar effect, far more modest than the star's, but nonetheless detectable. In principle, gravitational microlensing can reveal planets throughout the Milky Way.

Astronomers using this technique now have projects underway that observe the brightnesses of millions of stars, observing them every night in two different colors to make sure that any changes arise from gravitational microlensing. Of all the effects that might vary a star's apparent brightness, only this microlensing affects both colors in the same proportion. By timing the duration of the event and measuring the increase in brightness, the astronomers can accurately estimate the mass of the object producing the microlensing.

The microlensing project has led to the detection of several dozen microlensing objects, each with a few tenths of the sun's mass. These results establish the practical usefulness of gravitational microlensing, at least for detecting objects with considerably more mass than even a giant planet's. Within a few years we may reasonably expect that gravitational microlensing will reveal objects with masses comparable to Jupiter's, one percent of the sun's mass, or even less.

Interferometry

To make direct detection of Earth-like planets, as opposed to the giant, Jupiter-like planets that have already been discovered, many astronomers believe that we must send into space an interferometer, a system that combines the radiation detected by two or more telescopes to produce a single image whose angular resolution matches that of a single telescope as wide as the greatest separation of the individual telescopes. This means that so far as angular resolution goes, we can create the equivalent of a telescope with a mirror a hundred yards wide by constructing an array of much smaller telescopes spaced over a hundred-yard interval–provided that we maintain the distances between the telescopes to better than one hundred-thousandth of an inch.

If we do build such an interferometer system, it should look for planets by observing radiation from the infrared region of the spectrum, where a sunlike star will outshine an Earth-like planet by "only" about a million times, rather than by a factor of a billion, as it does in visible light. Because the interferometer tends to emit its own infrared radiation that will lessen its ability to detect faraway objects, we must cool the system to hundreds of degrees below zero, reducing this problem to manageable amounts. Furthermore, we must send the interferometer system out to four or five times the Earth's distance from the sun, because the zodiacal light, the sunlight reflected by interplanetary dust, shines so brightly in the inner solar system that we cannot hope to find Earth-like planets. Thus the futuristic plans for an interferometer that will do the job envision a system to be sent close to Jupiter's orbit, capable of maintaining amazingly fine alignment there, and of relaying data to Earth and obeying commands by radio. If we can design, construct, and operate such a system, we have a reasonable chance not only of finding Earth-like planets in orbit around sun-like stars, but also of using spectral observations to determine the surface and atmospheric characteristics of these planets, which affect the details of how the planet reflects and emits infrared radiation. Both NASA and ESA (the European Space Agency) envision such a system in operation during the end of the first quarter of the twenty-first century, as close to us now as the year that Richard Nixon resigned the presidency.

Planets Around Pulsars

We have saved for last the second method to yield success (so far!) in finding extrasolar planets: pulsar timing. This approach has revealed planets where no one expected them—around the collapsed cores of stars that have undergone violent explosion.

Pulsars are the product of rapidly rotating neutron stars, stellar cores that collapsed at the ends of their nuclear-fusing lives, squeezing themselves into fantastic objects that pack more mass than the sun's into a region no larger than a city. The collapse that forms a neutron star triggers a tremendous explosion, called a supernova, which blows the star's outer layers into space at speeds of thousands of miles per second. Such an explosion would surely destroy any planets that might have existed around the star, perhaps for billions of years before their destruction. Yet astronomers have found persuasive evidence that at least one pulsar, 1,600 light years from Earth, has three planets in orbit around it—planets with masses similar to, or even less than, the Earth's. These are by far the least massive objects ever discovered outside the solar system, and the only known extrasolar planets with Earth-like masses.

Discovery of these planets relied on the fact that because pulsars are driven by the rotation of the neutron stars that produce them, they emit pulses of radio waves at extremely precise time intervals, equal to the neutron stars' rotation periods. By carefully timing the pulses from some of these objects, astronomers have found cases where pulses arrive first a bit sooner, then a bit later, then a bit sooner again than would be expected from the average interval between pulses. They conclude that these variations arise from variations in the distance to the pulsar, and that the distance changes because the pulsar is moving in a small orbit, tugged first in one direction and then in another by the gravitational force from a companion object. The changes in the pulse arrival times reveal both the orbital period (the time for a complete cycle to recur) and the velocity with which the pulsar moves in its orbit around the center of mass of its system.

The most stunning success of this pulsar-timing approach appears in observations of the pulsar called PSR 1257+12, which emits pulses 161 times per second (the actual average interval between pulses equals 0.0062185319388187 second). Superimposed on this basic period of pulsation are small, cyclical changes in the intervals between successive pulses. Detailed analysis of the pulse arrival times shows that PSR 1257+12 has three objects in orbit around it, each pulling on it and affecting the distances that the pulses must travel to reach the Earth. These three objects have masses of 3.4, 2.8, and 0.015 times the Earth's mass, and orbit at distances of 0.36, 0.47, and 0.19 times the average Earth-sun distance, respectively. (These masses may be somewhat larger than these values, if our line of sight to the pulsar system does not coincide with the plane containing the objects' orbits, but the true masses are likely to be no more than two or three times the numbers given above.)

Astronomers know nothing about the physical appearance of these objects, though they strongly suspect they must consist mainly of heavier elements such as silicon, oxygen, carbon, and aluminum, and that they must have formed after the supernova explosion. The lightest elements, hydrogen and helium, should have been expelled into space by the supernova explosion, leaving no chance for the postexplosion surroundings to form gas-giant planets. Our prejudice may hinder calling these objects planets, but planets they seem to be, with the masses and orbital sizes of planets familiar to us, as they orbit the collapsed core of an exploded star. Though these planets may be Earth-like in terms of their masses and orbits, we can hardly expect Earth-like conditions on these planets, in terms both of what the planets look like and of the radiation they receive from their parent "star."

Nevertheless, the planets around this pulsar might—just might—harbor some form of life. How can we turn the "might" of speculation into the power of known fact? Only by detecting life unambiguously. In our solar system, such unambiguity may be slow to appear, given the difficulty in defining life, and in testing for it, to the satisfaction of all. When we look across interstellar distances, however, the test becomes simpler, for we cannot hope to find microbial life, or any form of life that lacks public relations skills. The issue of finding extraterrestrial life then elides into the more exciting question: How can we find extraterrestrial civilizations?

LIFE ON PLANETS BEYOND THE SOLAR SYSTEM

Planets around other stars attract the public, not because we love to think about planets as objects but because we love to dream about life on other planets. This dream, tied to our emotional longings and intuitive feelings about the universe, sets a high threshold to the level of public interest in a newly discovered extrasolar planet: If life won't fit, the hell with it. With only modest exaggeration, astronomers will tell you that no one talks to them for long without raising the all-too-human question: What do you think of the possibilities of life in the universe?

This elevation of life to the center of public interest in the cosmos actually has an even narrower focus that is consciously stated. Those who ask about life in the universe understandably have little interest in the overall possibilities for life, especially for life so distant from Earth that we have no possibility of any interaction with it. What counts to our inner selves are extraterrestrial forms of life that might visit—or probably have done so and will continue to do so—right here on our home planet. The fact that modern thoughts toward astronomy concentrate on the possible or likely existence of other forms of life marks an enormous deviation from past centuries of public opinion, which regarded the Earth as the only locus of life in the cosmos. Some things do not change, of course, including the intuitive feeling that the Earth forms the center of the universe, and that any other entities must surely seek to examine and to visit us, to fulfill their good or evil purposes.

In stark contrast to our intuition (we have reached the final opportunity for me to beat this particular drum), scientific analysis of life on Earth suggests that life should be abundant elsewhere in the universe. The living creatures we know consist of cosmically abundant elements, found throughout the Milky Way and beyond. Modern theories of how life began assign its origin to natural processes, and attribute the fantastic variety of life forms we see today to the power of natural selection.

These conclusions imply that life should exist wherever Earth-like raw materials and environments exist, and that the struggle for reproductive success, which we call natural selection, should lead to the evolution of a wide variety of organisms in any such environment.

Superiority of Planets and Carbon

Where are those environments, and how can we examine them? We must pause to evaluate our biases: We live on a planet and tend to look first to other planets to find other forms of life. We, and all the other life forms we know, consist of complex molecules, whose intricate structures depend on the ability of carbon atoms to link into long chains. Are we falling prey to an Earth-centered, human-centered prejudice when we state that extraterrestrial life most probably exists on other planets, and consists of long-chain carbon molecules?

Apparently not, if we include "large satellites" in the category of "planets." If we define life as collections of organized systems that possess the capacity to reproduce and to evolve, then planets offer the best places to find the right mix of ingredients to create complex molecules, along with the conditions most favorable for the interactions of these molecules. We can hedge our bets with proper scientific accuracy by saying that by concentrating on finding carbon-based life on planetary surfaces, we shall maximize our chances of success, and may later turn to additional sites, and other chemical bases for life, which deviate more widely from what we believe will prove the norm.

Of all types of atoms, carbon ranks first in its ability to form complex molecules by combining with other types. Carbon atoms can form bonds with one, two, three, or four different atoms, a flexibility that most other atoms lack. Each hydrogen atom, for instance, can bond with only one other atom at a time. Oxygen atoms can combine with one or two atoms, but not with three or four; nitrogen atoms can bond with one, two, or three atoms, but not with four. The reasons for these differences lie in the structure of different atoms, described by the quantum-mechanical rules that govern how the electrons in an atom orbit its central nucleus. These rules make carbon nature's favorite atom in its ability to form chemical bonds with up to four other atoms at a time.

Silicon can match carbon by bonding with as many as four other atoms, but they make extremely weak "backbones" for long-chain molecules because the bond between two silicon atoms has only about half the strength of the carbon-carbon bond. Equally damning for silicon is the silicon atom's affinity for oxygen, which tends to lock silicon together with oxygen for astronomically long times, as is the case with the silicon-oxygen (silicate) rocks on Earth. When we ally these insights to the fact that carbon atoms far outnumber silicon atoms in the universe, we shall not be surprised that carbon serves as the dominant atom in life on Earth, all of which relies on molecules made with a long chain of carbon atoms to whose sides other types of atoms attached themselves. In contrast to these carbon backbones, any molecular chains based on the chemical bonds between silicon atoms are inherently unstable.

Planets and the Requirement of a Liquid Solvent

Every form of life on Earth consists of one or more cells—sacs containing water, the "solvent" in which larger molecules float freely. As a solvent, water plays at least three crucial roles: It offers molecules the chance to encounter one another; it protects large molecules against changes in the temperature, which would otherwise break them apart; and its surface tension—the solvent's tendency to form droplets—must have once helped to organize something akin to living cells, long before true cells with enclosing membranes had evolved.

Water appears to be nature's finest solvent, though not the only possible one. Hydrogen chloride (HCl) could make a usable solvent, but because chlorine ranks far down on the list of cosmically abundant elements, it is hard to imagine a world where life relies on hydrogen chloride as its basic fluid. Among the possibilities for cosmically abundant liquid solvents, the six most abundant elements (hydrogen, helium, oxygen, carbon, neon, and nitrogen) can produce only three likely liquids: water, ammonia (NH_3) and methyl alcohol (CH_3OH).

Like water, ammonia and methyl alcohol might prove good solvents for living creatures, though water wins the head-to-head competitions. Of these three types, water molecules have the highest surface tension; they also furnish the best buffer against temperature changes, because it requires more energy to change the temperature of a gram of water than one of ammonia or methyl alcohol. Furthermore, water is likely to be significantly more abundant that ammonia or methyl alcohol on any Earth-like planet, because water probably forms the most abundant liquid that can freeze and melt in any planetary system. Ammonia and methyl alcohol do have the advantage of remaining liquid at temperatures that turn water into ice, but water remains liquid at higher temperatures than the other two potential solvents.

As biologists musing on extraterrestrial life have recognized the importance of a liquid solvent for life, our solar system has shown us that water can exist as a liquid even in regions where we might not expect it to do so. For example, we have seen that the frozen surface of Europa may conceal a worldwide ocean, kept liquid by the tidal flexing of Europa's interior. When we contemplate other planetary systems, it is easy to imagine that they too might have objects heated by tidal flexing from their neighbors. This would allow the possibility of liquid water—or of other liquid solvents—far outside the regions where starlight heating naturally maintains the proper temperatures for liquid water.

The first extrasolar planets discovered around other stars orbit so close to those stars that no water, methyl alcohol, or ammonia can exist as a liquid. (Furthermore, these planets are almost certainly gas giants like Jupiter, and lack any solid surfaces on which liquids can collect.) Only keen pessimists, however, expect this to be true of all extrasolar planets. Since the closest, most massive planets are the easiest ones to find by the Doppler-shift technique, it seems entirely likely that many less-massive planets orbit farther from their stars than the first dozen extrasolar planets. In short, astronomers, along with most of the public, find it entirely possible that billions of stars in the Milky Way—perhaps a sizable minority of our galaxy's 300 billion stars— have planetary systems, and that many of these systems include one or more planets with roughly Earth-like conditions, including the possibility of liquid solvents and an abundant supply of carbon and the other types of atoms from which living creatures can assemble themselves.

This spiral galaxy, cataloged as NGC 6744, about 30 million light years from Earth, resembles our Milky Way and contains several hundred billion stars. Will we ever discover how many of these stars have planetary systems, how many of those systems have produced forms of life, and how many of those forms have reached at least our stage of technological development?

How to Search for Life on Extrasolar Planets

So what's the problem? Why haven't we found these hypothetical, widely distributed forms of life? First, of course, we may note once again that our only hope for discovering life on extrasolar planets with anything like our present technology is to discover advanced civilizations, capable (by the working definition of "advanced") of communication across interstellar distances. If we hope to achieve this goal by finding intelligent beings with whom we can communicate, we must begin by abandoning our ingrained concept that we occupy a special position in the universe. We would certainly have an easier search if extraterrestrial visitors routinely came to Earth, and we should not ignore this possibility. But in utter contrast to what many people believe, no reports of such visitors inspire much confidence, because they possess the grave defect of relying on that most unreliable of recording instruments, the human brain (see the discussion of the Face on Mars in Chapter 7).

Whether or not we shall eventually find reliable evidence of extraterrestrial visitors to Earth, formulating a plan to search beyond Earth for our cosmic neighbors seems worthwhile. In implementing any such plan, however, we almost immediately face a significant obstacle. The vast depths of space may contain monsters or angels, beings unlike or like ourselves, but the search to find them involves formidable, inter-linked amounts of time, effort, and money.

These difficulties in searching for extraterrestrial life arise from exactly the same facts that make extraterrestrial life likely. Enormous amounts of space embrace immense numbers of possible sites for life—and also separate these sites by distances utterly unfamiliar to human experience. If a rocket trip to Mars takes a year, a journey to the closest stars at the same speed will require about a million years, since they are about a million times farther away. Since no one suggests building a rocket ship to embark on a million-year journey, if we choose to seek other civilizations we must either wait for a vast improvement in our technological abilities or use the fast-moving means of communication that nature has provided: electromagnetic radiation.

Light waves, radio waves, and all other forms of electromagnetic radiation travel at the same speed, about 186,000 miles per second, the fastest speed at which we can hope to send any types of signals. On Earth, we already use radio waves for communication (for example, all long-distance telephone calls travel by radio) because they are fast and cheap; in space, the advantages of radio are tremendous. We may send a spacecraft to Mars, but we command it and receive its results via radio waves, which take only a few minutes to travel the same distance that the spacecraft covers in a year. The spacecraft may cost a billion dollars, while the radio transmissions, even though they travel at the speed of light, cost just a few cents.

Scientific hopes for finding other civilizations rest on the assumption that they use radio as much as we do, and in particular that they generate large amounts of radio power in the course of their ongoing operations. Radio stands out within the full spectrum of electromagnetic radiation because cosmic objects produce relatively little radio power, and also because radio waves cost less to produce than other types of radiation such as infrared and visible light. The current scientific efforts aimed at detecting another civilization hope to find that civilization's radio signals, either signals deliberately beamed into space as beacons or (and here we face a far more difficult task) signals used for internal communications, on which we can "eavesdrop" with sensitive antennas and receiver systems.

Other things being equal, radio waves from another civilization will be detected more easily if the civilization is close to us. Radio waves spread out as they travel through space, just as light waves do, with the result that their intensity decreases in proportion to the square of the distance they travel. Any civilization attempting to receive radio or any similar messages from a civilization in another star system, or to eavesdrop on its internal communications, must deal with the weakening of the signal caused by the huge distance from the source to the receiver. We have now acquired the ability to detect a civilization that uses radio waves in much the same way that we do out to distances of hundreds of light years, which include millions of nearby stars. Of course, we have no guarantee that these putative civilizations employ radio waves or anything that resembles them, or that they still let their radio "leak out" instead of channeling it more efficiently in systems that resemble our cable television. In view of these problems, plus the overarching uncertainty about where to look among the hundreds of billions of star systems in the Milky Way, the challenge of finding intelligent life at astronomical distances seems daunting indeed.

To scientists involved with SETI (the *s*earch for *extra*terrestrial *i*ntelligence), these are the challenges that make life worth living. They have struggled with the issue of how to search for other civilizations, and think that they have the most reasonable answer. They have grappled with the techniques of search, and believe that they can overcome the most difficult issue, one that would not occur to the general public: where to tune the radio dial to find another civilization. They have confronted the most fundamental problem of scientific activity, how to obtain funding; when the United States Congress removed SETI from the budget, scientists involved in the project found private donors who allowed it to continue. Today, Project Phoenix, managed by the SETI Institute in Mountain View, California, performs an ongoing search for extraterrestrial civilizations, using telescopes in Australia, Puerto Rico, and the continental United States. The scientists involved in this search naturally stay current with the latest news about extrasolar planets.   They hope someday that planet-finding astronomers will announce not simply the discovery of a planet around a sunlike star but the finding of an Earth-like planet at an Earth-like distance. That planet will immediately become the center of all searches for another civilization by radio waves. And if it should happen that such a planet has life, but that life has evolved "only" to the point of intelligent dolphins, whales, and octopi that have no use for radio waves, then we shall have to try harder and wait longer for success.

If the Project Phoenix search, or any similar effort, had already produced a demonstrable signal from another civilization, readers would have heard a good deal more about it. Since the search has so far continued without such a momentous result, and may continue without success at least into the next millennium, we may well take a moment to ask ourselves: How much are we prepared to invest in the search for extraterrestrial intelligence? In 1993, the United States Congress made the decision insofar as taxpayers' funds are concerned: zero. Rather than urging my readers to help correct this misjudgment, either by contacting members of Congress or by making donations to SETI researchers, I congratulate them on finishing this book, thereby investing in an overview of the planets in our solar system and beyond. May your investment pay enormous (psychic) dividends, and may we find the opportunity to talk to some of our cosmic neighbors. If they awe us, OK; if we awe them, OY!

Further Reading

Brandt, John, and Chapman, Robert. *Rendezvous in Space*: The Science of Comets.
New York: W. H. Freeman, 1992.

Chandler, David. *Life on Mars*. New York: Dutton, 1979.

Cooper, Henry S.F. *Evening Star: Venus Observed*.
New York: Farrar, Straus, and Giroux, 1993.

Frankel, Charles. *Volcanoes of the Solar System*. Cambridge:
Cambridge University Press, 1991.

Goldsmith, Donald. *The Hunt for Life on Mars*. New York: Dutton/Plume, 1997.

Goldsmith, Donald. *Worlds Unnumbered: The Search for Extrasolar Planets*.
Sausalito, CA: University Science Books, 1997.

Goldsmith, Donald, and Owen, Tobias. *The Search for Life in the Universe*.
(3d ed.). Sausalito, CA: University Science Books

Kolb, Edward. *Blind Watchers of the Skies*. New York: Harper & Row, 1983.

Krupp, Edwin. *Echoes of the Ancient Skies*. New York: Harper & Row, 1983.

Ley, Willy. *Watchers of the Skies*. New York: Viking Press, 1963.

Morrison, David, and Owen, Tobias. *The Planetary System* (2nd ed.).
Reading, MA: Addison-Wesley, 1996.

Norton, O. Richard. *Rocks from Space*. Missoula, MT: Mountain Press, 1994.

Rogers, John. *The Giant Planet Jupiter*.
Cambridge: Cambridge University Press, 1995.

Sagan, Carl. *Pale Blue Dot: A Vision of the Human Future in Space*.
New York: Random House, 1994.

Shostak, Seth. *Sharing the Universe: Perspectives on Extraterrestial Life*.
Berkeley, CA: Berkeley Hills Books, 1998.

Weblinks

Astronomical Society of the Pacific:http://www.aspsky.org

Planetary Society:http://planetary.org

Astronomy Net:http://www.astronomy.net

Jet Propulsion Labratory:http://www.jpl.nasa.gov

NASA:http://www.nasa.gov

Astronomy Magazine:http://www.kalmbach.com/astro/astronomy.html

Sky and Telescope:http://www.skypub.com

Scientific American Library: The Planets features fly-bys of the surfaces of all the planets in the solar system, a planet building simulation game to test the laws of the universe, a 3-D interactive planetary museum, and a desktop planetarium to view the sky at any time from any place on earth.

Contents
Scientific American Library: The Planets
CD-ROM Discs for Windows® and Macintosh®

System Requirements
Windows®
PC with 486DX2/66MHz or higher processor
8MB RAM
1MB available hard disk space
SVGA graphics (256 colors with 640 x 480 resolution)
Double-speed CD-ROM drive or faster
16-bit sound card
Mouse or compatible pointing device
Windows® 95

Macintosh®
Macintosh or Power Macintosh® with a 68040/25Mhz or faster processor
13" or larger color montior (256 colors with 640 x 480 resolution)
8MB RAM
Double-speed CD-ROM drive or faster
System 7.0 or later

Technical Support
For last minute changes and trouble-shooting information, please read the README.TXT file located in the root directory on the CD-ROM. Please visit:

http://www.byronpreiss.com/techsupp/

for online Technical Support. If you need further technical assistance, please e-mail:

techsupport®byronpreiss.com, fax 212-633-0332 ATTN: Technical Support, or call 212-886-2340. Please address any questions regarding this product to welcome®bpmc.com or write:
Byron Preiss Multimedia Company
24 West 25th Street
NY, NY 10010
http://www.byronpreiss.com/

Installing *The Planets*

Windows 95
1. Insert *The Planets* disc into your CD-ROM drive.
2. Click Start, then select Run from the menu.
3. Type your CD-ROM drive letter and type:\setup. For example, type d:\setup if your CD-ROM drive letter is D.
4. Click OK and follow the on-screen instructions for installation.

Macintosh
1. Insert *The Planets* disc into your CD-ROM drive.
2. Double-click *The Planets* CD-ROM icon on your desktop.
3. Double-click the *Install the Planets* icon and follow the instructions on screen.

Starting *The Planets*
Please note that *The Planets* disc must be in your CD-ROM drive during use.

Windows 95
1. Click Start, select Programs, then select *The Planets.*
2. Highlight and click the icon for *The Planets.*

Macintosh
1. Locate *The Planets* folder on your hard drive or other location specified during installation.
2. Double-click *The Planets* folder, then double-click *The Planets* icon.

Exiting *The Planets*

To exit this title, click the square Control button on the lower right corner of each screen, and then click Quit. Click Yes when the Quit dialog box appears.

How to use *The Planets*

Main Menu

Click the icons for the Virtual Solar System, the Observatory, the Planetary Traveler, and the Planetary Museum to go to that section of the product. Click the general Control button on the lower right corner square above the Index button to access any section, go to help, turn the sound on or off, or quit the title. Click the Index button to select the index.

The Solar System Kit

- To make the planets orbit around the sun, click Run. To adjust the orbits of the planets, click Orbit.
- In the Orbit dialog box, select a planet by clicking any one of the planets in the white squares to adjust its orbit.
- Retrograde and Prograde determine the direction of the planet's orbit.
- Show Paths turns off the gold orbital paths in the Solar System Kit.
- In the Planet Kit, adjust the sliders and click Make Planet to create a new planet.
- Click Add to bring the planet into the Solar System Kit.
- The Close button will return you to the Solar System Kit.
- Click any one of the icons in the top row to try to populate your planet.
- Go to the Solar System Kit to make the planet stable enough to support life.
- Adjust the sliders to create a habitable atmosphere.

The Observatory

- Select the location and date of the night sky by clicking the Location button.
- Use the Animate Starmap dialog box to make the planets move across the sky. The planets' speed can be increased in one hour increments. Step advances the planets incrementally.
- The Reference button takes you to Fred Schaaf's *Seeing the Solar System*.
- Zoom changes the percentage of the sky on your screen.
- Time and Date allows you to view the sky at any point in the future or past.
- View lets you center the screen on any of the planets and turn on and off the constellations.

The Planetary Traveler

- Use the arrows located above and below the column of icons to choose a movie.
- Click the icon to begin the movie.
- The first movie in the right column is an interactive journey over the surface of Venus. While viewing this movie, use the directional controls to navigate your flight.
- All other movies are linear.

The Planetary Museum

- Click Museum Shuttle for a guided tour.
- To view one of the chapters, use the directional controls to enter any of the Galleries and navigate through them.
- Roll over the schematic map on the left to preview topics in the Gallery.
- Click the Gallery window to be taken directly to any panel.